The Last Harper

Julian Atterton is a young writer of great promise. He lives with his wife in a remote house on the North Yorkshire Moors and spends his time writing and researching into medieval history. He has studied at the Sorbonne in Paris and at the Universities of Cambridge and East Anglia. His interests include rock climbing, archaeology and acting.

JULIAN ATTERTON

The Last Harper

Richard Drew Publishing
Glasgow

First published 1983
by Julia MacRae Books

This edition first published 1987 by

Richard Drew Publishing Limited
6 Clairmont Gardens, Glasgow G3 7LW
Scotland

British Library Cataloguing in Publication Data

Atterton, Julian
    The last Harper. — (Swallow).
    I. Title II. Series
    823′.914[F] PR6051.T79/

    ISBN 0-86267-184-1

Set in Chinchilla by John Swain & Son, Glasgow
Printed and bound in Great Britain by
Cox & Wyman Ltd., of Reading

To my father

Contents

In the late sixth century the north of Britain was a jigsaw of small Celtic kingdoms. The warlords who ruled them were so busy fighting each other that when the English settlers of the east coast began to push westwards they were able to overrun the Celtic kingdoms one by one. It was a time of such chaos that little was recorded and the story of much of what happened in those years is now so wholly forgotten that it cannot be unearthed.

One of the few people of whom enough is known to form a small picture is Urien who ruled a kingdom called Rheged which stretched down the west coast from Galloway to the Estuary of the Dee. He is remembered because he tried to join together the broken kingdoms to defeat the English advance. He is remembered, above all, because he had a harper named Taliesin whose songs about him survived long enough to be written down centuries later in Wales, long after Rheged itself had vanished.

This is the story of how those songs first came to be sung.

N

.... Roman Roads
⌐⌐⌐⌐ The Wall

GLOSSARY

BRYNEICH: Caer Brighid — Yeavering Bell
Dun Guayrdi — Bamburgh
Isle of Metcaud — Lindisfarne

RHEGED: Caer Lugualid — Carlisle
Caer Legion — Chester

DEUR: Catraeth — Catterick
Caer Ebrauc — York

Outigern's Ride

It was late in the summer, the month of the bramble, and the clearest of mornings. My father and I had walked from the hill of the king's rath to a high rounded hilltop from which we could look down on the lands of Bryneich and the pale sea. To the north we saw the plain of the river Tuid, but to the east and south, and over the hills which rose ever higher behind us, the lands of our people, the Votadini, stretched as far as the eye could see. Across the valley of the Till I could see the hilltop settlement of Dod Law with its barley terraces and grazing sheep, and on the valley floor between us the forests of the king's hunting runs and the clearings golden with corn approaching the harvest.

The hilltop was one of my father's favourite places. He would take me there on summer days, with his harp in the calfskin bag he hung from his shoulders, and teach me the songs of Bryneich. It was only the first summer of my teaching, for in my early days I was plagued by a breathing sickness which made it seem unlikely that I would live to be a harper and follow in my father's footsteps. Now, in my eleventh summer, I at last had the strength to puff my way behind him as he climbed the hills, and the strength to make my voice climb in search of the high notes of the melodies he sang so clearly. I remember how the song he made me sing that morning was a song of the harvest, and I finished it flushed with pride at having reached all the notes. My father was lying back in the heather, his hands behind his head, and he smiled at the clumsiness of my fingers on the harpstrings as I ended the song.

'To hear you reminds me of my own voice when I was young and even slower on the strings than you,' he said. 'And yet there is something of your mother's voice in your singing, something good.' He chuckled. 'You'll have a fairer voice than your father, though there are those who would say you could certainly sing no worse.'

I did not laugh with him, for I had just seen something strange enough to fill me with a cold intuitive fear. Away to the east, a column of smoke was rising into the sky. At first it was a white thread, but even as I watched it darkened to grey then to black and began to drift thickly out to sea on the breeze.

'Father . . . ' I said.

The tone of my voice made him sit up sharply, turning to look in the direction of my stare.

'By all the rivers! That's Dun Guayrdi. Dun Guayrdi is burning.' He watched silently for a moment, then took the harp from my hands to slip it back into its bag. 'We must get back to the king's rath.'

He began to stride across the heather, so urgently that it was all I could do to keep up with him. At last we reached one of the trackways winding over the hills to Caer Brighid and could walk more easily. In front of us the column of smoke hung black on the distant wind, and as we reached the shoulder below the rath we saw people on the ramparts pointing and staring.

'Is it an attack?' I asked.

'It must be,' said my father.

'Is it the Sea Wolves?'

'That is my fear.' We had begun the steep climb to the gateway, and he spoke breathlessly, his eyes on the ground as though he were talking to himself. 'It is late in the summer for the Sea Wolves to strike, and three summers since they last came to Bryneich. We gave them hard battle then, and they were so glad to leave it seemed they would not return, but perhaps three summers can breed a whole new wolf pack. It could always be the Goddodin come cattle-raiding, but they rarely ride when there is a good harvest about to be gathered and we should have heard before now if they had crossed the Tuid. . . . It can only be a fire lit by the Sea Wolves.'

We passed through the gateway and into the rath to find that a crowd had gathered on the level space between the two summits of the hill. The men were clustered round Outigern the king while the women looked on from the doorways of the bothies. The king was speaking, the sun flashing from the old golden torc around his neck. Three warriors had mounted their horses and now they rode past us, through the gateway and down the hillside. The other men dispersed in different directions and Outigern, looking round, saw my father and came towards us.

'So, Talhearn,' he said, 'you have seen that the Wolves are with us again?'

'Then they have forgotten the mauling we gave them when they last made that mistake,' said my father.

2

'Or remembered how many of our warriors and sons the giving of the mauling cost us.'

The king and my father gazed into each other's eyes; it was as though they were saying more with their eyes than they could with words, and the intensity of it was as frightening as the column of smoke on the horizon. After a long moment the king broke his gaze and looked towards the high hills.

'I have sent riders to muster the war host; to muster, that is, as many as we can just before harvest-time.'

'It is cunning of the Wolves to come now.'

'High cunning,' smiled Outigern. 'Still, let us hope they count too much on my old age and dead sons. We will strike quickly, before they get too far inland. I have called the host to muster at the circle of stones at sunset, so we will be at Dun Guayrdi for tomorrow's dawn.'

The king's words ended in a sigh which could almost be of sadness as he and my father both looked east to where the column of smoke still guttered thickly upwards, staining the blue of the sky. I looked up at them, watching the breeze tug at their hair. They seemed so calm, as though nothing remained to be settled, yet through me there raced a sensation of dizzy speed as though I were running down a hillside or gasping for breath. I followed them as they walked down to the king's hall, where Outigern paused in the doorway and gestured at the harp slung from my father's shoulders.

'Remember that fine song you wrote for me after the battles of three summers ago? Let us hope tomorrow gives you reason to write some new verses to add to it.'

'Let us hope,' said my father, 'that tomorrow brings a whole new song.'

The king laughed and passed through the doorway. We walked round the hall to our bothy, which lay just above the ramparts on the valley side of the rath. Smoke was curling up through the chimney-hole and I caught the smell of broth simmering on the hearth. As we bent through the doorway my mother looked round from the fire and ran into my father's arms. I noticed the whiteness of her knuckles as her hands grasped my father's shoulders.

'They say you will ride tonight,' she said.

'And ride back tomorrow night,' said my father. He kissed her hair. 'And now we are hungry.'

3

The evenings were shortening but still long. Outigern called his warriors early to the feast-hall, and I sat outside in the late afternoon sunlight, watching the shadows lengthen on the sides of the hills. Inside the hall I could hear laughter and my father singing hunting songs.

When I looked towards the coast I saw only a thin white plume where the dark smoke of the morning had been, but when I looked west towards the low sun I saw warriors riding the tracks of the high hills. Some turned north, heading for the valley of the circle of stones, but many came to the rath, leaving their horses by the gateway and striding into the hall where they were greeted by shouts. Some of them I had seen before at the gatherings of the great feasts and knew by name; Mael whose cattle filled two valleys. Fernvael the Fat whose daughters were said to be the most beautiful maidens in all Bryneich, and the warriors, Ciaran and Cuil One-Eye, heroes of old war trails of whom my father told many stories. The hall grew full and the women bustled to and fro with food and mead.

Slowly the sun dropped until the hills were a dark mass, until only the gateway side of the rath glowed in the amber light, and it was then that the warriors came out. They filled the level space between the summits of the hill as they mounted their horses, their arm-rings and necklaces of pale gold glowing in the twilight. Outigern the king passed first through the gateway, and I ran to the rampart to watch as the others streamed after him down the hillside, the hooves of their horses drumming against the turf. I watched the folds of their cloaks billowing from underneath the round white-painted shields of poplar wood they carried slung from their shoulders, except for my father who carried his harp. I watched until I could hear them no more, until they reached the edge of the valley of the circle of stones and were swallowed up by the trees and the gathering dusk.

The skies changed in the night, and the next morning there were clouds blowing in from the west, their shapes echoed by the shadows they set rolling over the hills. From our doorway I could see to the coast, but there was no column of smoke, no sign of any kind. It was simply the view I had known every day of my life.

On the ramparts I saw Uaran, a boy of my age but stronger, the only warrior of any kind left in the rath. He was leaning on a spear and staring to the east and I could tell he would have given anything to ride with the men of the war host. I joined him and

4

asked if he had seen anything, but he only shook his head and gazed towards the sea. After a while, seeing that I was still there, he spoke, but without looking at me.

'They may still be chasing the Sea Wolves, hunting them down after the battle.'

'Will we be able to see them coming back?'

'It depends where the hunting takes them.' He shrugged. 'If they take the forest tracks I won't see them till they cross the valley floor. They'd still be an hour away . . .' he nodded his head at the rath behind us, . . . 'enough time to tell the women to start their cooking.'

I looked round at the hall and bothies of Caer Brighid. The silence was unsettling. Usually when the men were away hunting the women made the rath their own and would sit outside to comb and braid each other's hair. Today they were invisibly busy; my mother had set off alone to the stream below the rath with a basket of washing. The fear of the day before came back to me and I turned to Uaran.

'Why are the women so silent? Is it that they do not think our warriors will return?'

Uaran's head jerked with surprise as he turned to look at me. He met my eyes, then looked away and back to the sea.

'When the Sea Wolves came three summers ago,' he began, 'I watched the riding of the king. There were more men with him than there were last night. My father and my brother rode with him, but they were not alive on the day that he rode back, nor were the king's sons. It was a day for women to weep, that one, and now they are afraid they have come to another.'

I began to hope against hope that my father would come back, It was as if I had spoken aloud, for Uaran took one hand from his spear and laid it on my shoulder. 'Don't worry. Your father will return, singing about it if I know him.' He gave me a thin-lipped smile. 'Listen. I'll keep watch on Dod Law, and you watch the valley.'

It was late afternoon before we saw riders, and we saw them on Dod Law. Two horses approached the settlement, and even at such a distance they seemed to be moving unusually slowly. An hour later a group of seven came out of the trees on the valley floor, riding fast through a cluster of fields. They carried the white shields of the Votadini but they were not coming to Caer Brighid; they turned north and galloped out of our sight towards the valley of the Tuid. We knew then that something was wrong.

We searched the forests below with our eyes, then after what felt like a year we saw one rider come out of the far trees and cross the valley floor, heading straight towards us.

We waited until we saw his shape through the trees beneath us, riding round the flank of the hill to climb to the gateway, then we ran around the ramparts, Uaran calling to the women to gather. As we reached the gateway our faces turned west for the first time that day; I noticed that the clouds had joined and darkened over the high hills, and knew we would have rain with the evening.

The women gathered uneasily by the king's hall while Uaran and I stood in the gateway watching the rider gentle his exhausted mount up the steep slope to the rath. Only when he was near to us did he look up, and I recognised my uncle, Cialgrin the smith. He hardly saw me; he rode past with hollow eyes, his left hand on the reins, his right hand hanging bandaged and limp by his side. His horse came to a stop in the centre of the level space where the warriors had mounted. He looked around him once, swallowed, and spoke softly.

'Outigern is dead . . . the men of Caer Brighid fallen with him . . . the Sea Wolves hold the coast. . . .'

His voice tailed away. There was a moment of silence, then the air was filled with wailing and sobbing as the women began to keen. Beside me Uaran dropped his spear to the ground and sat down on the grass, shaking his head from side to side. I thought of my father and turned emptily to look up at the hills he had loved. Even as the tears came I realised I was standing on the same spot where, the night before, I had watched what I now knew to have been the last riding of the Votadini of Bryneich.

The Ghost Road

The rain came just before sunset, and when late that evening I burrowed into the striped blanket and crushed bracken of my sleeping corner it was still falling hard, soaking our turf roof so that in three places rain dripped and splashed onto the floor of the bothy. I was far from sleep and lay in a waking nightmare winter forest where baying wolves ran through the trees.

It was my uncle, Cialgrin, who had said that wolves were baying, when he gathered us into the king's hall, empty now of its warriors and hounds, to hear what he could tell us. He had told of how that morning the riders of the Votadini had been beaten back and cornered against an outcrop of rock by a host of Sea Wolves with heavy axes, how one by one Outigern and his warriors had fallen, my father among them, and how now their bodies lay in a birch thicket within two arrow-flights of Dun Guayrdi.

'We knew when we first saw the Sea Wolves this morning,' he said, looking round at the empty tables of the hall, 'that this was no raiding party. They are led by a king. He lives tonight, knowing that he has spilt the last royal blood of the Votadini and that there is no life left for our tribe. His warriors will be hungry for land. We cannot stop them. We can only leave Bryneich as soon as we can or within days we will either be dead or slaves.'

I lay under my blanket wondering where we could go. I had never in my life been far from the king's rath, and when I had heard men speaking of the lands beyond Bryneich their talk had held no meaning for me. Now I listened hard as my uncle sat talking with my mother at the hearth of our bothy. He leant against the wall with his head back and his eyes shut as my mother cleaned the deep gash in his sword-arm and poulticed it with healing herbs. My uncle's face was lined with exhaustion and my mother's was as white as a full moon.

'Surely we could be safe if we took to a steading in the high valleys?' asked my mother.

'Perhaps for another two summers or so,' he replied. 'You should have seen how many young men they had in their war host. All of them will be wanting land of their own before they are much older. We have lost our struggle for this land of our fathers; the best we can hope for is a new life amongst a free tribe with a strong king.'

'I am not going to throw myself at the feet of the Goddodin.'

'I would not ask that of anyone, not with Morcant as their king and so many old wars between our tribes. They won't be crying for Outigern. No, we must go west over the mountains.'

'Over the mountains . . .' repeated my mother wonderingly.

'There is only one country where we would be welcomed as kin, and that is Gwynedd.'

'But that's almost the other end of Britain! Why should we be welcome there?'

Cialgrin sighed. 'Talhearn could have told the story better than I; it's an old one, though it is the beginning of the story that ended today. Long ago, before Artos, when the red fox Vortigern was high king, our king here in Caer Brighid was named Cunedda. He was a fine warrior, but over-playful in his cattle-raiding south of the Wall, and for that Vortigern sent him and the best of his warriors to Gwynedd to protect Caer Legion and the rich belly of Britain from the raiders of Eriu. That same summer Vortigern gave land at the mouth of the Aln to some of his Sea Wolf mercenaries, believing as he did then that they would obey him more readily than our king. Ever since, the people of Gwynedd have had no need to fear the raiders from Eriu and the people of Bryneich have had the Sea Wolf poison that has taken until today to kill us.'

'If this all happened before Artos,' said my mother, 'then it was so long ago that I do not see why the people of Gwynedd should even remember us.'

'Because of Talhearn and the harp-kind, because they still know of Bryneich in their songs even if they have never seen it.' My uncle smiled bitterly. 'It is said that exiles carry with them the sweetest memories of their homeland.'

For some moments my mother said nothing, sitting with her hands on her knees looking at the smouldering peat fire which she had kept alight later than usual to ward off the chill of the rain.

'And how would you reach Gwynedd?' she asked at length.

'It would be long,' nodded Cialgrin. 'We would need to follow the ghost road south to the Wall, and follow the Wall west. That would take no more than half a moon, then we would go south to Caer Legion, and from there west along the coast to Gwynedd.

That would take at least another moon, but with luck we would be in Gwynedd before the winter sets in.'

'And how would we pay for this journey? We have lived as members of a king's household, you as Outigern's smith and I as the woman of his harper. We have nothing to sell.'

'I can find us the horses, and you forget what it is to be a smith. I have never yet found a place which has not been grateful to give me food and shelter in return for my craft. I can do enough for you and the boy to be welcome also.'

'So the journey would be only for the three of us? You forget that I have sisters who have also lost their men and who have smaller children than Gwion.'

'No,' said my uncle, 'I had not forgotten, but I know what I can and cannot do. I can take you and Gwion, out of the love of my brother which goes also to you, but I cannot take half the tribe. It would be hard enough for the three of us.'

My mother fell silent. The wind outside was growing in strength and was now so loud that the rain could only be heard in the hollows between squalls.

'The decision is yours,' said Cialgrin.

'And a hard one,' she said, 'but I know my will in this. I do not wish to leave either Bryneich or my kin. Ride without me, but take Gwion and be a father to him. I will stay with my sisters and melt into the hills, and if in a few summers the Sea Wolves have us working their homesteads I will at least know in my heart that Talhearn's son is free.'

'This is really your will?'

'Yes,' said my mother. For the first time that evening her face lost its blankness and a sad smile lifted the corners of her mouth. 'You are tired and you must sleep. We will talk more in the morning.'

My uncle needed only to stretch out to fall into a sleep of blind weariness. I listened as his breathing grew deeper, watching my mother move about the bothy. She came towards me and I shut my eyes and pretended to be asleep. I heard the rustle of the bracken as she knelt beside me, and felt her breath on my face as she bent down to kiss my forehead. I opened my eyes but she was already walking away. She pulled back the door-curtain, and the last thing I remember as sleep pressed down on me is her figure silhouetted in the doorway as she stood staring out into the rain.

It was still raining the next morning, only harder, as if the skies were weeping for the fall of Bryneich. I awoke with a tight chest, breathing in shallow gasps; the lung sickness was with me again. It eased quickly, my chest began to clear, and I was able to sit by the fire and eat the bowl of hot oatmeal my mother had prepared. My uncle had gone, and my mother sat on the other side of the hearth mending a calfskin bag which I knew must be for my journey. The moon-paleness of the night before had left her, but it left her face set hard, like that of a figure carved in wood.

She began to tell me I would be leaving. She told me that my uncle needed help on a long journey and that even before the Sea Wolves came it had been planned that I should go with him, to travel the way my father had travelled when he was young. She spoke so softly that it was hard to hear her voice above the rain. I watched the set of her face, listened to the words I knew were a changing of the truth, and sensed that if this were the only way she could find to do things, the only way to help would be to act as though I believed her.

'When will we come back?' I made myself ask.

'With the spring,' she said, her face showing nothing.

But she showed everything in the way she clung to me when, the next morning, the clouds having spent themselves, my uncle and I stood with a mare and two ponies in the gateway of the king's rath. I was to ride one of the ponies, the other was laden with the tools of the smith's trade Cialgrin was taking with him; I had overheard him telling my mother how he had dumped a small fortune in weapons into the Till, so that rust and not the Sea Wolves should have them. No-one saw us leave except my mother and Uaran, who leant on his spear keeping his thoughts to himself.

As we rode through the flock of sheep grazing on the shoulder below the rath I looked back. My mother raised her arms upwards and I waved in reply. When I next looked back she had vanished among the bothies. As the distance grew, all I could see of Caer Brighid was the smoke curling upwards from the hearths and the sunlight shafting down on the roofs through the broken clouds. It became simply one of the hilltops over which we were riding, and I was so struck by all I had lost and was leaving that I could not bear to look back any longer.

I turned to face the trackway that wound ahead. My uncle rode in front, leading the pack pony. We were soon higher on the hills than I had ever been before, dipping down into valleys only to climb a further hill beyond. By midday we were climbing the slopes of Yr Cerrid, so called, my father had told me, because it lay like a great sow on the horizon as one looked west from Caer Brighid. Its sides were brindled with heather passing its bloom and bracken beginning to redden and dry, and they seemed endless as we slowly neared the rounded summit.

As we reached the top we rode into a full west wind that slammed into my chest, stealing my breath, and which made the manes of the ponies stream and ripple in the air. A whole new land opened up beneath us; curling away to south and west was an endless roll of hills, while to our north lay the wooded upper valley of the Tuid and the far hills of Manau Goddodin. My uncle halted his mare and gestured to me to ride to his side.

'We would have stopped here to eat, but it would be no rest in a wind like this.' He reached into one of the saddle-bags behind him and found a barley bannock which he broke in two to hand me half. 'So we'll eat in the saddle. We still have to ride the ridge to that hill there before we go down into the valley.'

I nodded and ate into my bannock, as there is nothing quite like a cold wind to make me hungry. We began the long ride down the far side of Yr Cerrid, which was now all I could see if I turned back.

By the time we left the ridge to follow a track down into a small valley widening to our south, I was frozen by the wind and aching from the long ride. The steps of the pony seemed like blows on my spine, and the change of sound as we left the high world of the wind sent waves of sleep washing over me. To keep myself awake I listened to the sounds of the valley, the rushing of the stream, the birdsong, and finally the bleating of the sheep as we came through a thicket of rowan trees to see a small cluster of bothies on a flat tongue of land made by the curling of the stream.

As we rode into the steading three women came out of the bothies and greeted my uncle by name. I could tell by the faces of two of them that either their men or their sons had fallen with the king. One of them, with eyes as green as apples, came beside me and said: 'You are Talhearn's cub. I saw you sitting by your father at the Beltane feasting.'

I tried to dismount, but somehow I just toppled sideways and crumpled into a heap on the grass. My uncle was beside me in an instant and lifted me up so that I dangled from his arms. I heard him telling the women about the wind on the tops and I felt myself being carried into a bothy and lowered onto a bed of bracken,

11

but I think I was asleep before they had time to wrap a blanket round me.

I had never woken in a strange place before, to see someone other than my mother tending the hearth fire. It was the woman with green eyes, and as I sat up she looked over and began to ladle me a bowl of hot oatmeal. I ached in every bone of my body, and despite the kindness of her smile I sat by the fire feeling sick and miserable. My oatmeal was hardly finished when my uncle came in.

'So you have woken after all,' he said. 'We thought you had curled up like a squirrel for the rest of the winter.'

Soon afterwards we took our leave of the steading. My uncle gave the women a sickle from the bundles on the pack pony to help them with the corn they would be harvesting without their men. I rode dizzily and painfully as we began to climb out of the valley, back towards the high ridgeway and the track through the winds.

We followed the ridgeway for the better part of the morning, making slow progress against the wind, and were coming down from a peak when we had our first sight of the straight road. It ran up from the lowlands to the north and I could see it tracing a line over the hills to the south. For a short distance it joined the ridgeway and followed it, and as we reached it the the bare earth of the trackway changed to firm flat stone under the hooves of our mounts. For all the length of it visible to both north and south there was not a traveller to be seen. I kicked my pony forward to go beside my uncle.

'Is this the ghost road?' I asked.

'That is what we call it now. It is one of the roads built by the Romans.' He was having to shout against the wind. 'They ruled here long before you were born, long before I was born, and they built these roads for their legions.'

'Before Artos?'

'Oh yes. There are even those who say that Artos was the last of the Romans. He used this road when he came north to fight in these lands.'

As the ghost road left the ridgeway track we turned south with it, so that only one side of our faces was frozen by the wind. My uncle leaned over.

'We have left the tracks of the Votadini now. It will be roads like this which lead us all the way to Gwynedd. They are wide enough for you to ride beside me.'

12

They also made for faster travelling. We were soon trotting down into a high valley where the empty walls of a Roman rath gaped at the sky by a ford in the stream. We ate there, barley bannock and some blackberries my uncle had been given by the women of the steading, then set off up the hillside beyond.

I was still too sad and battered to enjoy the journey, but the road, stretching in front of us as straight as a spear-flight, stole my thoughts and almost made me forget my bones. I imagined Artos and his companions riding south after their battles with the Sea Wolves, the Red Dragon banner of Britain flying at their head. Then I remembered how Artos, in the end, had lost, so I tried to imagine instead the Romans who had built the road and how large their war hosts must have been to need such trackways.

Late in the afternoon the wind ceased and the clouds flattened and joined into a roof over our heads. The sky to the west lost its grey and began to glow like the Midwinter fires, and I realised that as the road turned to follow a stream down towards a wooded valley beneath us, we were turning to ride west into the sunset. My uncle, who held the reins with his left hand as his sword-arm hung beside him, looked at the sky too and smiled to himself. I remembered one of the songs my father had taught me, a song with a tune that was high and skirling like the birds of the hills who had been our only company that day, and suddenly I found myself singing it to the sky.

> 'I am a stag of seven fights
> I am a flood across a plain
> I am a wind on a deep lake
> I am a tear the Sun lets fall
> I am a hawk above a cliff
> I am a thorn beneath the nail
> I am a wonder among flowers
> I am the wizard — who but I
> Sets the cool head aflame with smoke?'

I paused, trying to remember the words that followed.

'Go on,' said Cialgrin.

'I can't. It's as much as I know.'

'So Bryneich's songs die with it,' he muttered. His eye was caught by something ahead of us. 'See, another rath of the Romans.'

13

It stood on a flat-topped rise above the valley floor, larger than the rath we had passed earlier that day, and it was alive with the shadows of twilight by the time the road had led us to where a gateway cluttered with rubble broke its long walls. We drew rein and looked in.

'We won't disturb the ghosts,' said my uncle. 'There's a story that a king of the Votadini fell in battle here. We'll make our camp down there on the edge of the trees.'

We spent the last of the daylight preparing for the dark. Cialgrin vanished into the woods to set hunting snares to see if the night would bring us any meat for the following day. I scampered about, gathering and laying the wood for a fire, heaping the fallen leaves and dying bracken to make two sleeping places, seeing to the horses and making myself too busy to feel alone and afraid.

After we had eaten we pulled our cloaks about us and sat by the red pool of the fire. I watched my uncle's face in the glow, seeing in it echoes of my father's that I had never noticed before. My uncle was watching me and I wondered if he were thinking the same.

'I'm sorry I have no harp,' I said.

'So am I,' he said. Then he looked at me from under his brows. 'What did your mother tell you of our journey?'

'She told me little, but I heard you talking the night before.'

'Then you know as much as I do. What are your thoughts on going to Gwynedd?'

I stared into the fire. 'I do not have any. I can only think of what has happened. I cannot imagine Gwynedd.'

'But you sang for the sunset,' said Cialgrin. 'Until this evening I felt nothing but shame at not having fallen with the men I had known all my life. I had no wish to run in search of lands I have never seen. That changed when you sang. I knew again how good it is to be alive, to hear singing, to see beauty in a sunset and to know you will see others.'

We sat silent for a while, then my uncle took a last look at the horses and we curled up in our sleeping places.

3

Urien of Rheged

The end of our third day on the Romans' road brought us to the Wall. We approached it across a wide flat moor, slackening our pace as we drew nearer, refusing to believe it could be nothing but an empty rampart whose towers held only rotting parapets and the odd birds' nest. We held our breath and rode through the ruins of a square Roman rath where the wind squealed through the crumbled buildings. As we came out of the far gateway we turned off the road, which dropped away south towards a wide valley, and took to a track which ran along the rim of a large ditch which followed the Wall as it stretched westwards over the hills.

We slept that night in the bothy of a shepherd; a small, dark man who asked no questions and showed no interest in answering any my uncle put to him, but who gave us good mutton stew, a barley bannock and a bowl of curds in return for some spearheads from my uncle's bales. He was about to take his sheep down off the hills for the winter, and the one thing he did tell us was that we would be lucky to meet anyone at all on the higher hills further west.

He was right. The next morning we followed the Wall down into a sheltered valley in which we saw a few herdsmen watching the rust-coloured cattle who matched the falling leaves and the hills above, but once we had left it we saw no-one. The Wall snaked from crag to crag, broken only by the mouldy little forts which all looked the same. We knew there were people in a long valley which lay to our south, but here on the tops it was an abandoned world. We could see the remains of small steadings where plots of land had been cleared and cultivated. All I could think was that, when the Romans left, the few who remained had felt themselves too heavily outnumbered by the ghosts to care to stay long.

The afternoon brought rain, and after a couple of hours we were too wet to think of anything but the cold in our bones. We reached a large Roman rath on a sloped hilltop and searched it for some corner with a steady roof that would give us a dry night. Eventually we found one outside the ramparts amongst a huddle of bothies which seemed to have been lived in long after the rath itself had been abandoned. It was filthy and stank of sheep, but there was a pile of dry firewood in one corner. My uncle took a bag of beans and spat one into each corner to silence any lingering spirits, and I made a fire. By nightfall we were sitting by the hearth as the rest of the beans stewed in a pot and our cloaks hung steaming from the rafters.

By the next morning the rain had quietened to a drizzle, but a thick white mist had fallen, muffling sounds and hiding the world. We had noticed the day before that a road came up from the valley to the gateway of the rath, and we found that it continued alongside the Wall to our west. All day we rode along it, seeing nothing but a spear's throw of trackway stretching ahead of us into the whiteness, knowing nothing of what lay to either side of us, and hearing nothing to tell us anything.

We knew we were reaching the end of the afternoon when the mist began to darken around us. The horses slowed, as though afraid of the ever-thickening curtain of invisibility. I turned to my uncle.

'Where are we going to camp tonight?'

'We should come to a track leading off to some rath or tower on the Wall. Let's hope that wherever we end up there's a roof as good as last night.'

'But it's getting dark.'

'And we are getting nearer, so be patient.' He smiled at me, but as he turned his eyes back to the road ahead I saw something in the knit of his brows which reminded me of the look my father's face had worn as he watched the burning of Dun Guayrdi. We rode on, while the mist around us turned to dark grey.

Suddenly, ahead of us, we heard hooves approaching. We stopped to listen but there was no sound except for the spluttering of a burn somewhere off to our left. After a moment we nudged the horses forward again. I said nothing; I was too busy listening. Then, very close by, a horse snorted loudly. We could still see nothing. I looked at my uncle.

'Ride on,' he whispered, 'as though you've heard nothing.'

So we did. I tried to concentrate on looking and listening but my thoughts flew everywhere. If we were attacked we were helpless; I had no weapon and Cialgrin's sword-arm hung bandaged beside him. I prayed fervently to all the gods I could remember, but the prayers froze in my head as I saw the horsemen.

They were nothing but silhouettes. Two men with spears sitting silently on their horses, and beside each horse a hunting hound. They were quite still, and they blocked the road in front of us.

'Are they Roman ghosts?' I asked my uncle.

One of the horsemen burst into laughter, and together they cantered towards us out of the mist, the hounds bounding beside them. The one who had laughed swung his spear-tip earthwards in a greeting of friendship, and my uncle and I found ourselves being looked over by a pair of eyes greyer than the mist.

'We are no ghosts,' he said. 'I am Owain ap Urien, and my companion is Geraint ap Riwal. And who are you, and why might you be riding the high road to Rheged so late in the year?'

The fall of darkness did not bring the wet night on a hillside which the mist had threatened. Instead I found myself sitting by a large fire eating rich venison stew. The two strangers had led us to a place on the Wall where a signal tower had kept its roof and invited us to share it with them for the night. They had been hunting earlier that day and the carcass of a deer hung from the rafters. As they cooked they told jokes about how in the mist they had all but ended up hunting each other. Only after we had eaten, as we sat back from the fire and the hounds stretched out, did Owain ask my uncle to tell our story.

I listened as my uncle told of Outigern's ride, how the lost battle left Bryneich open to the Wolves, and how he and I had crossed the hills, but I noticed that he did not tell them we were heading for Gwynedd. When he had finished, Owain spoke.

'We had heard before of the Wolves clinging to your coast. We call them the Eingl. We had heard they had a strong king, and were thirsting for land, but we hoped they would ride south and take it from the men of Deur, who are no friends of ours. I'm sorry it was north that they turned.'

'We knew they would come,' said Cialgrin. 'It was the last battle of an old war I have known all my life. They used to raid every summer, then three summers ago we broke them in battle. When it was done we knew it would be our last victory, for it left us with so few young men. This time when they came we knew it was only to make an end of it. . . .' I remembered the look that had passed between my father and the king and understood why I had felt that they spoke less than they knew.

'And when the end was made,' said Owain softly, as though finishing my uncle's words for him, 'you had nothing to stay for.'

Cialgrin nodded.

Owain stretched his legs. 'It has been a summer of blood in Rheged also. You will have heard of the fall of our king?'

'Gwendolleu is fallen?'

'In the early summer. The kings of Deur came through the passes on a cattle-raid. I was in the far south with my father and half our war host. We had had wind of an attack from Gwynedd and Powys which never came. When we returned we found the kind dead, the cattle stolen, and much of the land wasted. They came too early to wreck the harvest, but we've had a busy summer trying to rebuild all they did wreck.'

'Why the men of Deur?'

'Why indeed? We have never troubled them. Gwynedd and Powys are our old enemies. Five summers ago Rhun of Gwynedd marched straight through Rheged to Strathclud and we found ourselves being trampled into the dirt. We sent messengers to Peredur of Deur asking for help, as one would of an old brother, and his reply was to join in the raiding. There has been no love between us since, and that is why we were hoping the Eingl would chew his throat a little.'

'Why have you not harried Deur yourselves?' asked Cialgrin.

Owain smiled into the fire. 'It was always the hope of Gwendolleu the king that the men of Rheged and Deur might once more be brothers, and it was always his fear that if we took a war host into Deur, the kings of Gwynedd and Powys would lose no time in bringing their war host into Rheged. In his fear he was right, but his hope was the death of him.'

'We are too far from the Britain of Artos,' said my uncle.

'Ah, there will be no more stories like that,' said Owain. He leaned forward to put more wood on the fire. 'But Rheged has a new king, and will be stronger by the by. The time will come when the men of Deur, and even of Gwynedd and Powys, will be happy to be our brothers rather than our enemies.'

'I add my hopes to yours,' said Cialgrin. He rubbed his bandaged sword-arm. 'I have seen enough of fighting and travelling for the time being. I am a smith, and I want to turn my hands back to my work, so tell me if this new king of yours would be grateful enough for my craft to offer Gwion and me a hearth for the winter.'

Owain laughed. 'I'll ask him,' he said, 'he's my father.'

The next morning the mist had cleared, and the land I saw before me was quite different to the world of hills that had been my last sight before the clouds touched the earth. We had reached the edge of the hills, where the Wall ran down towards a wide plain with forests and farms through which rivers snaked towards a blue inlet which could only be the waters of the western sea. The sky was clear except for high clouds like tufts of sheep's wool and the wind blowing from the sea carried a taste of salt.

Geraint was readying the horses.

'What do you think of Rheged?' he asked.

'The plain and the sea remind me of Bryneich.'

'Then may it give you a second home,' he said. 'It is less than a day's ride to Caer Lugualid. Your journey will be over by nightfall.'

We set out towards the plain and had soon left the bare hillsides to ride among trees. It was high autumn; the leaves were amber and gold and constantly falling from the branches to be caught by the wind. We passed fields that lay bare after the harvest, and several burnt-out steadings that told of the raiding of the men of Deur. Owain and Geraint rode in front, their hounds loping beside them. The only one of us who took no pleasure in the ride was our pack pony, who had to carry the deer carcass as well as my uncle's bales of goods.

Towards midday we joined a road running south and left the Wall behind, then we rode through a village which had not been burnt. The forest surrounded us once more until we emerged onto riverside fields, beyond which were the ramparts of the biggest rath I had ever seen.

'Caer Lugualid,' called Geraint.

Its size was only the first of its strangeness. Once inside the gate the Roman road continued as straight as it had run over the bare hillsides by the Wall, only here there were houses down each side. Most of them were as large as the feast-hall of Caer Brighid, and all of them could have held our bothy seven times over. They were even cornered with small bricks as regular as the paving stones of the road. My uncle and I looked around in amazement. One thing made it eerie; there were so few people. We passed groups of men, women scurrying along with baskets or talking in doorways, and even small children chasing each other or making little heaps of stones, but for every house sending hearth smoke up into the sky there was another standing empty and roofless.

We entered a large flagged square where Owain and Geraint dismounted outside a building with foundations of Roman brick out of which rose the timbered structure of a feast-hall. Men came towards us and as my uncle and I dismounted they set about untying the deer carcass from our pack pony. Owain gestured to us to follow him into the building.

It was a traditional feast-hall, with hearths and tables and shields hung on the wall, but it had a beautifully paved stone floor across which we followed Owain to a doorway in the far wall which led into a walled courtyard. Shrubs grew by the walls, and had in places cracked the paving, but my eyes were held by a basin in which stood a stone statue with water gurgling out of its mouth. The courtyard was a place of stillness, or could be were not two men pacing up and down beyond the fountain locked in what seemed to be a quarrel.

One of them was bearded and gesticulating wildly as he talked. The listener could only be Owain's father, Urien the king. He had Owain's grey eyes and curling hair, only his was brindled with grey about the temples and round his brow ran the pale gold circlet of kingship. The bearded man finished a speech about his poverty with a wave of the hands which rattled several heavy bracelets he was wearing, and looked at the king expectantly. When Urien replied it was in a slow, steady voice, and he gestured with his eyebrows, not with his hands.

'I am not stealing your cattle,' he said. 'The men of Deur stole your cattle, Cadoc. I am asking you for the tribute I need to maintain a war host so that the men of Deur do not steal your cattle ever again.'

'But if I give you the number you ask for I will have none for them or you to take from me in the future. I am not one to refuse tribute, but I am worried for next spring in a farmer's way.'

'I am worried for it in every way,' said Urien. He glanced at us then back to the bearded man. 'Still, when I sent to you for cattle I asked from my memory of your herds, not from a knowledge of how things go with you. Stay and eat with me tonight, and tell me how the farming goes in the high valleys.' With that he turned to us. 'Owain, how was your hunting?'

'Good,' said Owain. 'I bring back deer for your table, and travellers with news of Bryneich.'

'Bryneich?' said the king, surveying Cialgrin and me with the same grey gaze his son had shone at us through the mist.

We sat down on stone benches in the far corner of the courtyard and my uncle told our story. A girl of my age came from the feast-hall carrying a bowl of mead with great concentration. As she handed it to Cadoc I stared at her hair; it was red-gold like burnished copper and trailed down the back of her dress like a cascade of flame. Cadoc drank and passed the bowl to Cialgrin, who broke off his narrative and took a long draught before passing it to me. I offered it straight to Owain, but he indicated that I should drink first. A sip was all I could manage. It was strong mead, with fire beneath the honey-sweetness, and it made me splutter, cough, and blush with embarrassment. Owain took the bowl from me with a grin and whispered something to the girl, who skipped into the hall and came back with an elm-wood cup of water with crushed mint leaves.

'This is my cup,' she said as she handed it to me, 'and this is what I drink. I find the mead too strong.' Laughter flickered in her eyes as she spoke, and she turned away to take the empty mead-bowl from the king and disappear into the hall.

My uncle had finished speaking.

'You ask me for a hearth for the winter,' said Urien, 'yet you do not speak of returning to Bryneich. Is it in your thoughts to leave next spring for Gwynedd, where you might find old kinsmen?'

I slid a look at Owain, who seemed startled at this. My uncle, however, merely nodded. 'When we left Bryneich it seemed that Gwynedd would be the only place to go. I did not tell your son this because he told me they were enemies of yours.'

'I won't hold your blood against you,' said Urien. 'I have need of a good smith and I could give you work for more than one winter. You are welcome here for as long as you wish to stay, and if you decide to move on you can tell Rhun of Gwynedd you made me many fine weapons which will sing for his blood if ever he troubles me. By the east gate of the city there are some old Roman shops and among them are two empty smithies. Take one of them to work and live in and eat at the tables of my hall. As to your work, you and I will talk again once you have settled.'

'That is a gracious welcome,' said Cialgrin.

'In the meantime,' added the king, 'you are my guests and you must be tired. Owain will tell you of a woman who can help heal your sword-arm, and now he will take you to the smithies.'

We rose and left the courtyard, as Urien and Cadoc resumed their talking behind us. In the feast-hall the women were preparing the hearths to cook the evening meal. I looked for the girl but saw her nowhere, so I set the elm-wood cup down on one of the tables and followed Owain and my uncle out into the square.

4

Winter Solstice

I learnt quickly the difference between Bryneich and Rheged. In Bryneich I had been Talhearn the harper's son and I knew almost everyone — in Rheged I was little Gwion and I knew almost no-one. The day after we came to Caer Lugualid, Urien the king rode out with his companions and Owain and Geraint rode with him. In Bryneich the autumms were long and dry — in Rheged they were drenched with rain. Cialgrin and I slept on the floor of the feast-hall, for though my uncle had quickly chosen the better of the two smithies in the dead street of shops, we could not live there as there was no roof.

Each morning we splashed through the wet streets to the smithy. My uncle had only one good hand to work with, and all I could do was fetch, carry, and clamber up onto the rafters to find out which were firm and which were not. They all were, luckily, and we spent several days collecting fallen tiles from the roofs of the nearby shops and fitting them together on the gaping rafters of our own. As the roof began to take shape, so half our floor began to dry and I realised that it would eventually be a snugger place to live than my turf-roofed bothy in Bryneich.

The woman who worked on the healing of my uncle's arm was called Fionn; a tall, sad woman who swayed like a willow when she walked. She had been bride to a man who had fallen with Gwendolleu in the early summer, leaving her with no children and an empty hearth, and she came to the feast-hall every evening to dress my uncle's wound with dark ointments that smelt of the forest. On the first evening she cleaned and salved it silently and went away, but on the second evening, when the king had gone and the hall had only the women and a few old men, she turned his wrist over and over, tracing and squeezing the heavy ridge of the gash with her fingers.

'The wound needs rest,' she said. 'It was well cleaned when it was new, and could heal to give you back your hand as strong as before, but you have ridden too far with it and now you work it too hard. You must give it time to mend itself.'

'How would you have me find the time?' said my uncle, though I could see from his face that he felt pain as Fionn

22

examined the wound. 'We cannot sleep on the king's floor all winter, and the hand has already been idle so long I have all but forgotten my craft.'

'The king might prefer a two-handed smith,' she replied. 'You will come and be the guests of my hearth until the healing is done.'

'That is gracious . . .' began my uncle, but Fionn had begun to salve the wound as if there was no more to be said.

After the meal she led us through the streets to where part of a large old house had been repaired with timber to make a two-roomed dwelling. A bright-patterned rug hung on the wall of the hearth room, one side of which lay empty where earlier that year a warrior's weapons had stood and his hound had slept. Neither my uncle nor I could think of anything to say. She laid out old mats and rugs for us to sleep on, and sat for a while on the far side of the hearth before taking to the next room where she would sleep. The flicker of the fire played light onto the rug on the wall and made it seem like a door-curtain blowing in a breeze. My uncle quickly fell asleep, but I lay awake long enough to hear Fionn sobbing softly in the night.

In the week before the feast of Samhain, the king and his companions rode back with the tribute of Rheged; a drove of cattle, pigs and sheep, followed by several wagons stacked with grain. In the feast-hall that night Owain made his way to where my uncle and I were sitting. He was accompanied by a boy who seemed no more than three summers older than me, and who looked like Owain but for a shock of red hair which reminded me of the girl of the elm-wood cup.

'I bring my brother Pascent to meet you,' said Owain. 'Tell me how you find Caer Lugualid.'

'We find it a place of kind welcome and the best of smithies,' said my uncle.

'Good,' said Owain. 'My brother would like you to make him a sword.'

I listened as Cialgrin asked Pascent about sword weight. As they talked I looked round the hall and caught sight of the girl with red hair serving the king. It was only as I realised she must be Owain and Pascent's sister that I realised Urien had no queen.

I found out more three mornings later when Pascent came to the smithy to choose between two blades my uncle had forged for him. My job was still that of fetching and carrying, but now it had stretched to keeping the fire. Keeping the fire meant bending over blinding heat as I worked the bellows, and my face and arms felt permanently scorched. Whenever I could I would go and stand in the doorway and let the rain splash onto me. Sometimes I was so hot the rain seemed to steam on my face, as if I were one of the old sun-heroes in the tales my father used to tell me when the breathing-sickness kept me to my bed, and often at night my head ached so badly that Fionn had to give me a potion of bitter herbs to make me sleep. I was standing in the doorway letting the rain soak me as Pascent prepared to leave.

'Do people from Bryneich always stand in the rain?' he asked.

'I'm not used to the fire.'

'Have you not always helped your father?'

'Cialgrin is my uncle. My father was a harper, and he died with our king.'

'It must be hard to be both fatherless and motherless.' Pascent pulled his cloak about him and leaned on the other side of the doorway, looking out into the street. 'At least you knew your father. I cannot remember my mother. She died when I was three winters old, when my sister was born.'

'Your sister?' I asked, thinking of the girl with red hair.

'My sister Branwen. Because of it my father loves her more than all his three sons put together.'

'I did not know there were three of you.'

He laughed. 'Aye, well, you may never meet my brother Elphin. Two springs ago he went and became a monk in the monastery at Hwitern. If ever you do see him return to eat at my father's table it will be a night to remember. I must go. . . .' He called goodbye to my uncle and ran off into the rain.

It was the eve of Samhain, the turning of the year, and in the evening we held the feast of the Dead. Empty places were left at the tables for the warriors who had fallen during the year, and there were many empty places. Fionn knelt by one of them, keening silently. I thought of Caer Brighid and wondered if the women were holding the feast in Outigern's hall, or if the Sea Wolves had burnt it down and left the hearths open to the sky.

The sombre meal was almost over when a tall cloaked man came into the hall. Several of the women gasped, and the men stopped talking. I stared and saw a gaunt-faced man with a straggle of beard. Underneath his cloak I made out the shape of what could only be a harp-bag.

'Myrddin!' exclaimed Urien, rising to his feet.

'My lord Urien,' said the tall man. 'You need not turn as pale as a rowan blossom. I come from the north, not from the underworld.'

'We thought you were dead,' said the king.

'And I am not, which is why I am here. I could not have you laying my place with the Dead, or the red lord of Annwn might send his hounds for me before I feel ready to follow them.'

'We heard you fell with Gwendolleu.'

'I did, with a spear of the Eingl in my left shoulder, but I was still alive in the morning. Two women healed me.'

'Then where have you been?'

'In the forest of Arderydd, waiting for the turning of the year.'

'And now you have come . . . ?' asked Urien.

'To take my place amongst the Living,' said Myrddin.

A place was set beside the king, and he and the tall man were soon deep in talk. The other talk in the hall came to life again and the feast drew towards its close. Fionn came over to where my uncle and I were sitting.

'I am going now,' she said. 'Follow when you wish.'

'Fionn,' said Cialgrin, 'the smithy is ready and my hand has healed. It seems the time to thank you for your kindness and to leave you to your hearth.'

She shook her head, and for the first time since we had met her a faint smile lifted the corners of her mouth. 'No, the year is turning and the Dead are gone. It is good that you live with me.' She rose quickly and left the hall.

My uncle stared after her. 'I think I'll make her a cooking pot,' he said.

With the passing of Samhain, autumn became winter. I had never been so conscious of the death of the year. The half-silent streets of Caer Lugualid seemed to echo it, and even if I ran round the ramparts or out into the forests, all I saw were bare trees raising empty branches to the sky. Fires were no longer simply for cooking, they were beacons of life, symbols of the energy that survives all. I came to love the fire in Cialgrin's smithy, and found joy in feeling the heat grow as I pumped in air from the bellows.

One afternoon my uncle told me to ready the fire while he went with one of Urien's companions to collect some old metal. I was alone in the smithy and as I gave the embers their first gust of the bellows a blow-back of acrid woodsmoke stung my eyes and made me cough. Squinting with the pain, I began again. All I could see through my narrowed eyelids was a band of glowing red, and I remembered how on the journey out of Bryneich I had ridden towards a band of sunset the same colour as the fire. I remembered the song, too, and as I bent over the bellows I found myself singing to the flames.

> 'I am a stag of seven fights
> I am a flood across a plain
> I am a wind on a deep lake
> I am a tear the Sun lets fall
> I am a hawk above the cliff
> I am a thorn . . .'

I got no further. I heard rapid footsteps behind me, then a hand gripped the neck of my tunic and dragged me to my feet. I screamed as I was slammed against the wall of the smithy. Hands gripped my shoulders and I found myself looking up into the quivering face of Myrddin the harper. He looked as though he had seen a ghost.

'Why do you sing that song?' he rasped.

I was too terrified to speak. He clenched his teeth and slammed me against the wall again.

'How do you come to sing that song?'

'My father . . .' I spluttered. 'My father taught it to me.'

'Who was your father?'

'Talhearn, harper to Outigern of Bryneich.'

Myrddin blinked, then let go of me and staggered backwards, almost falling into the fire. He leaned against the far wall and began to shake from head to foot. 'Forgive me,' he muttered. 'Talhearn . . . Talhearn ap Tataguen?'

'Yes.'

He shut his eyes and screwed them tight until he stopped shaking, then, looking around the smithy as though seeing it for the first time, he sat on a stool by the fire.

'Forgive me,' he said again. 'Talhearn ap Tataguen . . . I knew him. We met in Caer Ebrauc, in happier times.' He shook his head from side to side, then threw it back and laughed. 'You must think me mad. What are you called?'

'Gwion.'

'So. Do you know the meaning of the words you were singing?'

'The meaning?'

'Aye, the meaning in the words, the voice that is speaking. . . .'

I could not see what he meant. 'It is a song he was teaching me,'

I said. 'There is more, but I have forgotten it.'

He looked at me over the fire, then nodded. 'He would be teaching you the song first. The meaning comes later. Forgive my almost strangling you. That is a song only sung by harpers of the true kind, and it is weird to me to hear it on a boy's lips.'

'Is it forbidden to sing it?' I asked.

'No, no, but there is a time and a place for the singing of it. Your father would have told you. I cannot.'

I picked up the bellows and began to work the fire again, thoughts falling over each other in my head. After a moment I looked up at the harper. 'Would you teach it to me?' He looked at me but said nothing, so I went on, 'If my father had lived, and Bryneich had lived, he would have taught me his songs and I would have been the harper of the king's hall after him. Let you teach me the songs he did not live to teach me, so I may be a harper like my father.'

Myrddin looked up at the rafters. 'You could have a better life as a smith,' he said, 'and it takes many years to become a harper.'

'I am young. I have many years.'

He nodded, then slowly a smile began to twitch its way along his mouth. 'You are very young, and perhaps I will have the years to teach you.' He slapped his hands on his thighs. 'So be it, Gwion ap Talhearn. I will teach you all I know, and make you a harper.'

So it began. During the days I worked in the smithy with my uncle, making weapons for the war host of Rheged, and in the evenings I sat at Myrddin's feet and listened whenever he told the old tales to the people gathered in the feast-hall. From time to time he would pick up his harp and sing the words the heroes had spoken, then lay it across his knee and continue the narrative. I could close my eyes and travel with the tales, and I came to hate the moment when he ended and I had to open them again, even though they were met by happy faces I knew better with every day.

Each evening, as we sat against the walls of the feast-hall while the women prepared the meal, Myrddin would ask me to tell him the tale I had listened to him telling the night before. It was beyond me. I could remember the heroes with their deeds and misdeeds, but I could not shape them out of words and bring them to life. With time I learnt to catch small moments of each tale and store them away with all their richness, and this taught me patience, for I knew that one day Myrddin would tell the tale again and I would catch a moment more.

With the harp I learnt more quickly. My father had taught me well, and when Myrddin first grudgingly untied his calfskin bag and handed me his beloved, the feel of the polished oak and horsehair string was not of strangeness but of welcome. I played every day until my fingers quickened, and when I sang the hunting and harvest songs of Bryneich my father had taught me I forgot my voice and fingers and heard only the skirl of the music. Once or twice I ended a song to find that Myrddin had closed his eyes and the women had paused at their cooking, but usually I needed everyone's tolerance as I practised one ripple of a song over and over again before I could even make it bump like a stream over countless uneven boulders.

On the morning of the Winter solstice I was in the smithy when Myrddin arrived in one of his frequent wild-eyed moods. 'Get your cloak,' he said to me. Turning to my uncle he said: 'No helper for you today, Cialgrin. Greater magic calls.'

My uncle nodded good-naturedly. Both his hands were strong now, and besides, Myrddin was not a man to argue with. I followed the harper out of Caer Lugualid and turned with him to take the riverside path. He walked fast and the wind blew his cloak out behind him. The snow had not yet come, but there had been frost that morning; the ground seemed to creak underfoot and tears of ice clung to the long grasses that hung over the river. There seemed little point in asking Myrddin where we were going. He often disappeared for days at a time, and I only hoped he was not about to do that now, as I wanted to be back for the Midwinter feast in the evening.

We arrived at a bend in the river and Myrddin headed towards a copse of trees that stood alone on the bank, set apart from the rest of the forest. It was only as we reached them that I saw they were set within a circular ditch in which thin ice covered the water. From somewhere inside came the rustle of an animal darting for cover. Myrddin stretched his long legs over the ditch and I jumped it, then we passed through the trees and found ourselves in a circular clearing at the heart of the copse. I knew then that it was a sacred grove.

I stood in the centre and put my head back, watching the bare crowns of the trees leaning with the wind beneath the pale winter sky. My nose itched with the cold. When I looked down, Myrddin was standing at the base of one of the trees on the edge of the clearing. He beckoned to me and I crunched towards him across a tangle of fallen and long-rotten branches.

'Tell me the name of this tree,' he said.

I looked in bewilderment at the few saw-edged yellow leaves which still dangled from its branches and at the dark splits in its pale bark. The only trees I knew by name were oak and rowan, which grew around the foot of Caer Brighid.

'It is the birch,' said Myrddin, 'the first of trees.'

I looked around the grove. 'But there are other trees which look older and taller.'

'Are you a poet or a woodcutter?' groaned Myrddin. 'It is called the first of trees because four moons from now it will be the birch who first puts out new leaves to greet the spring. Now, how many moons are there in a year?'

I vaguely remembered a line in a song about loving someone until the thirteenth moon had come again. 'Thirteen?' I asked.

'Aye, thirteen,' said Myrddin. He gestured with his arm at the trees of the grove. 'Each of these moons is sacred to a different tree, and each of those trees gives its name to one of the thirteen months of the year. Tonight the year ends and the dark is at its longest. Tomorrow the new year is born, and tomorrow night and every night after that the nights will grow shorter as the year grows in strength. The first moon of that new year is the moon of the birch, which is one of the two sacred trees of birth.'

'Which are the other sacred trees?'

'That I will teach you as moon follows moon. All I will teach you now is a song.' He unslung his shoulder-bag and pulled out the harp, loping to the centre of the clearing as he fingered the strings. 'It is the song your father began to teach you.'

It was hard to think of learning. I was transfixed by the sight of the tall harper, swaying slightly from side to side, singing in the heart of the sacred grove; but when the words joined the music I forgot everything else.

> 'I am a stag of seven fights
> I am a flood across a plain
> I am a wind on a deep lake
> I am a tear the Sun lets fall
> I am a hawk above the cliff
> I am a thorn beneath the nail
> I am a wonder among flowers
> I am the wizard — who but I
> Sets the cool head aflame with smoke?

I am a spear that roars for blood
I am a salmon in a pool
I am a lure from paradise
I am a hill where poets walk
I am a boar ruthless and red
I am a breaker threatening doom
I am a tide that drags to death
I am the infant — who but I
Peeps from the unhewn dolmen arch?'

The song ended and the only sound to be heard was the wind in the tree-tops. Myrddin came towards me with a wild grin on his face.

'Now tell me,' he said, 'who is the singer of the song?'

I looked around the grove, half-hoping that the trees would whisper the answer to me, mumbling the lines of the song to myself and trying to make a pattern out of the images in the words. I could only admit how lost I felt. 'I can think of no god who has the power to make so many changes.'

I expected Myrddin to groan again, but instead he nodded. 'You're very close. The singer of the song is the one thing with the power to make so many changes.'

I stared at him blankly.

'Take it as a riddle,' he said. 'Who rushes in like flood and wind and ebbs away like a tide? Who gives a season to the stag, the hawk, the salmon and the boar? Who gives a time for spears and a time for poets?'

'The year itself?' I asked.

'The year itself!' shouted Myrddin. 'The song is the song of summoning, for harpers to sing tonight, at the Midwinter feast, to call the infant year out of a dolmen arch as yet unhewn.' His grin returned and he held out the harp to me.

'And tonight, you will be the harper who summons the new year.'

I have never enjoyed a Midwinter feast as little as I did the feast that night. The hall was packed with people who had come from all over Rheged. Myrddin sat at the high table with Urien and Urien's cousin Llywarch, the lord of southern Rheged who Myrddin had told me was a harper as well as a warlord. All I could think of was that I would soon have to sing to all these people, and my stomach tied itself in such tight knots that I could only pick at the roast pork and honey pastries, and shake my head gloomily whenever someone offered me the mead.

My time came soon enough. When the feasting was done Urien rose, lit a torch at one of the hearth fires and led the way out of the hall. In a few moments the edges of the square were lined with people holding torches, whose light made shadows dance on the dark heaps of the two unlit Midwinter fires which stood in the centre. Myrddin passed me the harp, saying: 'Remember, you are singing not to all these people, but to the goddess of Life who is giving birth to the year.'

I took the harp and stood between the two unlit fires. A priest Llywarch had brought with him was reciting a prayer, for this was also the birth-feast of the Christ-king, but as soon as he had finished Urien signalled to me to begin my song. I felt my fingers on the harp-strings and heard the music spring to life, looked up from the crowded square to see a black sky with stars like a thousand fires, then the song seemed to bubble up inside me and burst into voice.

Suddenly it was over. The people cheered and ran forward to light the fires with their torches, and to dance between them as they began to blaze. I took the harp to Myrddin. Urien was laughing, his hand on his cousin's shoulder, saying: 'It's many winters since your voice was as sweet as that.'

Myrddin kissed my forehead. 'Now go and eat something,' he said.

I moved through the dancers and the laughter towards the doorway of the feast-hall where my uncle and Fionn stood smiling at me. Before I could reach them, Branwen came to me with a bowl of mead. Her red hair flashing with the light of the fires and thin crescent moons of silver hung from her ears.

'Surely after that,' she said, 'you will drink some mead.'

I raised the bowl to my lips and drank until my whole body burned in its own Midwinter blaze.

'So,' she smiled, 'you like the mead of Rheged after all.'

'Lady,' I murmured, 'from your hands I would drink anything and love it.'

Owain and Pascent joined us. Pascent was so flushed with mead that his face seemed as red as his hair. 'Watch out, my sister!' he said, wagging a finger. 'He's a poet now, and poets have ways with words which could steal your heart.'

'All you have is a way with mead, and you're not getting any of this,' retorted Branwen, gliding off into the crowd.

'That was beautiful singing,' said Pascent. 'They must have

31

heard you over in Bryneich.'

My thoughts flew to Bryneich for the first time in days, and the fact that neither my father nor my mother had heard me sing made it all seem so meaningless.

'Well,' said Owain, 'I hope old Myrddin lets you sing to us more often.'

'Why should he?' I retorted. 'He is the harper to the king of Rheged. I have no king and no country.'

As soon as I had spoken I realised how rude and ungrateful I must sound, and I blushed. Owain simply nodded, then put one arm round Pascent and one arm round me and led us towards the feast-hall. 'When I am king,' he said, 'you will be my harper.'

5

Red Lleven

Three times the Winter solstice came and went. At the birth of each year I sang the song of summoning, and each year I understood more of its meaning. They were years in which the breathing sickness slowly left me, and they were years of learning. In the first winter Myrddin taught me the calendar of the trees and the symbols of the seasons. In the second winter he taught me how each tree of the calendar gave a letter to the bardic alphabet in which songs could be written down. In the third winter he taught me the ogham script, in which letters were transformed into mere cuts on the edge of a squared birch rod to make a message which only true harpers could read.

Through all these winters, as unbroken as the flow of a stream, lay the learning of the tales and songs through which a harper makes his living. The heroes and heroines became so well known to me that I could lose myself as completely in the telling of their stories as in the singing of a song. I learnt how to weave tales in and out of each other so as to entertain a feast-hall for as long or as short a time as wished. In the second winter Myrddin made me a harp of my own so I could both sing whenever I wished and sing in the feast-hall in Myrddin's place whenever he was away on his travels.

I never went far from Caer Lugualid. In the summer, when the king rode out with Owain, Pascent, Myrddin, and his companions, I was left to work with my uncle in the smithy. I never quarrelled with this, for when the men were away the women of the hall would call on me to sing away the long evenings, and at their centre was Branwen. My love for her grew with every moment I shared with her. She could read my eyes but never spoke of it, for the daughters of kings need not make any allowance for the emotions of harpers. It was enough for me to be near her, to drink from her beauty as though it were the elmwood cup she had once offered me and to share her ringing laughter. She laughed often, yet her favourite song was the saddest I knew, the lament of Deirdre for the sons of Uisliu.

There were days when Caer Lugualid itself seemed to call for a sad song. The more I came to know the city, the more its size amazed me. So many of its houses were empty and ruined and so many of its streets were silent. I would sit in the ruined places and try to imagine how they must have bustled in the days of the Romans, and how they must have shrieked when the Yellow Plague filled the gutters with the dead. The life of the city now was not its people but its king.

It seemed that whenever Urien returned it was in triumph. In the first full summer of his kingship he rode south to settle old scores. The war host of Rheged entered Powys and took Solomon, the king, prisoner in battle, leaving him with no choice but to sue for peace and promise alliance in the future. Rhun of Gwynedd did not wait for Urien to turn towards him, but sent gifts and bargained for peace. When winter came the two oldest enemies of Rheged had been humbled into promising to respect and guard its southern borders. In the second summer Urien rode north to visit Riderch of Strathclud, an old ally, and received from him a fresh pledge of friendship. The word of all this must have travelled east because the men of Deur kept to their own side of the Pennuin. In Rheged itself the cattle grew fat, the harvests were rich, and many children were born. One of them was a boy born to Fionn and Cialgrin, and suddenly I was no longer little Gwion but Gwion the uncle of little Dichuil.

The wind changed on a hot evening in the third summer, shortly after the barley harvest. The king had been visiting his own lands in the Lake Mountains to the west and he rode back unexpectedly to Caer Lugualid. While the women hurriedly found extra food for the cooking fires word spread round the city that riders were being sent out to muster the war host of Rheged. I made my way to the square and found Pascent among some warriors who were sharpening their weapons and repairing the rims of their shields.

'What has happened?'

'You have not heard, then? News reached us from Riderch that a war band of Eingl had been seen coming west over the hills north of the Wall. We don't know if they are making for Strathclud or Rheged but my father wants to teach them that it's poor wisdom to head for either.'

'Where are they from?'

He leaned back and ran his hand through the shock of red hair which the long hot ride had stuck to his forehead. 'It seems they are from Bryneich; the same breed, no doubt, who killed your king. Apparently they are making quite a kingdom there. They call it Bernicia.'

My heart began to hammer. 'I'm going to ask my uncle for a sword,' I said. 'This time I will ride with you.'

When I reached the smithy I found my uncle sharpening a sword; not a newly-made one, but an old cold grey weapon which I guessed had not seen daylight since Outigern's last battle. He took one look at my face. 'So you've heard the news?'

'Are you riding with the king?' I asked.

'Oh yes. I would not want to miss this for all the gold in Eriu.'

'Is there a sword for me?'

Cialgrin's eyebrows arched upwards in surprise. 'You are not a warrior, Gwion.'

'This is my fourteenth summer. Is that not the age when boys take their weapons and sit on the men's side in the hall?'

'In the old tales, yes, but even they are boys who have been trained to be warriors. Don't forget you were so weak a child your parents thought you might never see your fourteenth summer. You have never held a sword, you have never even carried a hunting spear. If you went into battle, even if you only fought a boy your own age who had been training with weapons since the age of nine, don't try to tell me you would live to sing about it.'

'What would you have me do?' I shouted. 'Sit here singing to the women while you are fighting the Wolves who killed my father?'

'It is hard, I know,' said my uncle, 'but that is what I would have you do.'

I ran out of the smithy feeling speechless with fury and did not stop until I had reached the feast-hall. I saw Myrddin and the king sitting at the high table and made my way to them.

'My lord Urien!' I burst out, causing them both to turn and look at me.

'Gwion,' said the king, 'you bring news?'

'I have come to ask for a sword. My uncle refuses to give me a weapon so I can ride with you and fight against the men who killed my father, so I ask one of you.'

The king's eyebrows arched as Cialgrin's had done, though a trace of amusement flickered at the corners of his mouth.

'You have no training as a warrior,' he said. 'You might as well ask me to kill you now, more cleanly than you would be killed in battle.' He gazed at me with his implacable grey eyes and I felt the fury ebb out of me to give way to helplessness. I swallowed my anger and lowered my voice.

'So you tell me to stay here with the women?'

The amusement left his face and I knew I had spoken too rudely. It was Myrddin who saved me.

'In the old days,' he said, 'the harpers never fought at all. They watched the battle and decided if it were worthy of a song. I have no wish to see you die when I have taught you so much, and if you cannot keep a cool head I will ask Branwen to keep you tied to a post while we are gone. However, I would ask the king to bring you if you promised to do no more than watch, as a harper may.'

'That I will allow,' said Urien. 'Your father was a harper. Avenge him with a song about our victory over the Eingl. Does that seem fair to you?'

I nodded my head. 'That seems fair to me.'

Two mornings later I rode out of Caer Lugualid with the war host of Rheged. My uncle gave me a weapon after all; not a sword, but a thin dirk as long as two hands and as sharp as a razor. He also gave me some grim advice: 'If the Eingl come near you, hide the dirk beneath you and lie on your face as though you are dead. If they turn you over, stab upwards into the stomach.'

There were privileges to being a harper. I rode beside Pascent near the head of the war host, just behind the Red Dragon banner of Rheged. We rode north through the forest, scattering the birds from the trees. I recognised a road which turned away to the east as the road which had brought me from Bryneich, but the war host kept to a road which headed north towards Strathclud. At the rath of Petrianis where we crossed the Wall we found Cadoc and a band of warriors waiting to join us. We rode on through the forests and cornfields of the plain until a rim of hills began to form a horizon to the north and east of us. I gazed towards them whenever there was a break in the trees, knowing it was somewhere among them that our search for the Eingl would lead us.

The search was short. We halted at midday by the banks of the river Lleven, Myrddin was telling me how we were within an hour's ride of the forest of Arderydd where Gwendolleu fought his last battle, when a rider came into sight on the track which followed the riverbank. He halted in surprise at the sight of the war host, then rode straight up to the banner which marked the place where Urien was sitting beneath an oak.

'Greetings my lord Urien,' he began. 'I was riding to find you.

The Eingl appeared last night by the ghost rath at the source of the river. This morning they began to move down the high valley, burning the steadings as they came.'

'How many are they?' asked the king.

'At least nine score.'

'Then we are well matched.' Urien looked round the war host then gazed into the smooth-flowing stream. After a moment he turned back to the messenger. 'Will they reach the plain before nightfall?'

'No, they have too few horses, but they will reach it tomorrow.'

Urien nodded, smiling as though it were the answer he had wanted, and raised his voice to address the host. 'The Eingl are high on the Lleven and burning their way downstream. We will camp tonight on the edge of the hills, and when the Eingl reach the valley mouth we will be there to make it the last place they ever see.'

We spent the afternoon following the river upstream, Owain having ridden ahead with a scouting party. We passed several small steadings which seemed to have only just been rebuilt and reoccupied after the raiding of the men of Deur three summers before. By the early evening we had reached the edge of the plain, where the river ran faster and more noisily, and where on either side of us hills rose up to form the lips of the valley of the Lleven. Owain was waiting to lead us to a forest clearing not far from the riverside track, and we busied ourselves with settling the horses and preparing a camp for the night. Above us the trees were heavy with the summer foliage and it seemed the most peaceful place imaginable, but a sense of suppressed expectation hung over the war host like the pressure of a storm about to break. I was glad when Urien gave the order for there to be no cooking fires; I did not feel like eating.

Scouts had been posted on the hills and three ruseful old hunters had been sent up the valley itself. They had already sent word that in the far distance they could see the rising smoke of burning steadings. For the war host in the clearing there was nothing to do but wait, and I would have been sick with the length of the evening if Myrddin had not called me to work. We told and sang the story of how Cu Chulainn of Ulster fought single-handed against the war host of Connaught, and by the time we had finished it was dark and the men dispersed around the clearing to sleep.

The night was warm and insects danced from sleeper to

sleeper. For a long time I lay awake, listening to the coughs of the sleepers and the noises of the forest, and trying not to think.

I was woken by my uncle as the night sky above the hills was paling with the approach of dawn. For a moment I had no idea where I was, then my memory returned and I scrambled to my feet. All around the clearing the war host was up and moving.

'Why don't you stay with the horses?' asked Cialgrin.

I shook my head. Myrddin loomed out of the darkness, his hair even more dishevelled than usual, and signalled to me to follow him. My uncle laid a hand on my shoulder.

'I'm following Owain onto the other side of the valley to you. The sun and the moon be on your path, and keep your head down.'

He vanished into the darkness and I realised for the first time what it was that we were about, and that I might not see him again. I followed Myrddin to where the king was mustering his band and we set off through the trees, stumbling over roots.

When dawn came we were settling into hollows, or behind boulders, in the woods on the southern side of the valley. Looking down through the trees we could see the empty riverside track, the river, and the wooded slope beyond on which Owain and his men were ensconced. My stomach was bubbling emptily and I felt weak and ill. The valley was unbelievably calm; the birds had accepted our presence and were in full song and there were even squirrels scratching along the branches of the trees. I knelt with Myrddin behind a mossy boulder a few feet from where Urien stood surveying the scene, looking for all the world like a hunting hound sniffing the air.

One of the scouts ran lightly through the trees and up to the king.

'They're on the move,' he said. 'They'll be here in less than an hour.'

'On the track?'

'Aye, and they don't even have scouts out ahead of them.'

'Good,' said Urien. 'Go tell it to Owain.' He looked at Myrddin and grinned, then fixed his attention on the valley once more. I closed my eyes in the hope it might silence the thudding of my heart.

'Look!' said Myrddin. I opened my eyes and followed his pointing finger. A hare had appeared on the riverbank. For a moment it sat motionless on a rock, then bounded out of sight upstream. Myrddin slapped his thighs and turned to the king. 'That's the best of omens. It means the battle will go our way.'

I shut my eyes again and wrestled with the knowledge that being a harper also meant believing in hares. The hour that followed seemed longer than the cruellest of winters. My legs were numb from my long crouch when whispers were passed from man to man.

'They're here.'

The riverside track was still empty but the birds had fallen silent. Floating down the valley came the sound of men singing. It grew nearer and became more distinct. For the first time I heard the language of the Eingl, and the singing was ugly and raw as though it sprang from the throat and not from the lungs. They came into view below us, a host of marching men with some three dozen riders amongst them, shields and heavy axes slung from their shoulders. My gaze was riveted by one of the horsemen, a tall man with a mane of tawny hair and a beard who wore a heavy mail tunic and who could only be their chieftain. The first of them passed in front of us and only when the whole host seemed to be beneath us did Urien turn to a man beside him.

'Now!'

The deafening blast of a hunting horn over-rode every other sound in the valley. The Eingl froze in their steps and stared into the trees with wide eyes as they tried to make out what was happening. The instant the wail of the horn tailed away the air whistled as from both sides of the river a shower of spears, arrows and slingstones rained down upon the raiders. Many men fell. All around me warriors were running down the slope and out of the trees. I saw Owain and his men break out of the woods on the far bank and charge through the river before the Eingl could get to the bank to hold it. I found myself alone amongst the trees while below me on the valley floor was chaos, a whirlwind of movement with its own tempest of sound . . . the yells and screams of the fighters, the ringing of weapon on weapon and the terrified squeals of wounded horses.

Slowly the chaos took on a pattern. Urien and Owain had joined up to make a semi-circle of warriors slowly pressing the Eingl into the stream. The Wolves tried time and again to set up a shield-wall but each time a breach was driven through it and they were forced backwards into an even smaller knot of fighters, stumbling over their own dead. The riders among them fought from the saddle, the tall rider with the tawny mane yelling encouragement to his companions and slashing with long sword-strokes at any man of Rheged who came close. As the band of Eingl around him grew ever smaller I saw Pascent snake in to the horseman's left. The rider swung and brought his sword crashing down, splintering Pascent's shield-rim and slicing into his arm. He screamed and staggered backwards and I lost sight of him in the press of warriors who moved forward to push the Eingl harder.

The tall rider began shouting to the few of his companions who were still on horseback. Somehow they moved together, their companions on the ground parting to let them through. As soon as they had grouped they rode at one end of the semi-circle of warriors of Rheged and hacked their way through. I saw Cadoc cut down by an axe. They broke out onto the trackway, but instead of attacking the men of Rheged from behind they galloped away upstream, heading for the hills.

The battle they left behind was a short one. The Eingl made a hopelessly brave last stand on the riverbank and were cut down one by one. When it was finished the Lleven was streaked with blood. The head-rattling clang of weapons ceased and was replaced by the groans of the wounded and dying and the gurgling of the river.

I made my way down through the trees, feeling dizzy at the spectacle of it all. The valley floor was a tangle of bodies. I found Pascent propped against a log with a gash in his shield-arm which Myrddin was binding with a strip of torn cloth. Pascent grinned at me.

'Did you see?' he asked. 'I nearly got their chieftain.'

'From where I stood it was the other way around,' muttered Myrddin. 'If you'd been a hand's breadth to the left your head would have gone flying.'

'I think his name was Aethelric, judging by what one of them shouted.'

Myrddin shook his head. 'The Eingl have such ugly names.'

Urien and Owain came over to us. 'We should not have left the horses so far away,' said Urien. 'Those riders will be half way back to Bryneich by now.'

'We could still hunt them down,' said Owain.

'No,' said the king, 'we'll get the wounded back to Caer Lugualid and be grateful there are so few.'

Several minutes later I set off for the clearing, walking slowly with Pascent leaning on my shoulder. I had seen all I wanted to see of the battle. We were almost there when I heard rapid and heavy footsteps behind us. I turned to see my uncle, his face a mixture of expressions — both grim and happy at the same time.

'I'm afraid I must ask you to forgive me,' he said to Pascent, who simply looked at him in bewilderment. 'You were cut down by their chieftain, weren't you?'

'Yes.'

'Well, I was near Cadoc at the place where they broke out. I got a good look at their chieftain. That sword of his which hit into you, I made it many summers ago for Outigern the king of Bryneich.'

The rest of the summer passed quietly. The corn harvest came, and was a good one. Whenever either Myrddin or my uncle set me free I spent the time with Pascent. His arm healed fast, and through the grace of Fionn and her arts the wound gave neither fever nor sickness, but he was used to riding and hunting, unused to wandering weakly around Caer Lugualid, and it must have seemed the longest summer of his life.

I would find him in the courtyard of the fountain surrounded by the maidens. There was one called Cairenn who made no secret of the place she kept for him in her heart. I would happily have stayed there, to be close to Branwen, but usually he took my arrival as the chance to go for a walk round the city. We would visit Fionn and laugh as Dichuil the brown-eyed bairn ran around the room flinging himself at everyone and everything, or we would lean on the ramparts looking down into the ruined gardens and pretending to debate which house Pascent should repair as the personal feast-hall of a prince of Rheged, or we would go through the north gate and simply sit by the river.

We were by the river one evening in the month of the bramble when Owain and Geraint galloped down the road as if the Wild Hunt were after them. They had left only that morning for what was to have been several days hunting, so we knew at once that something must be wrong. As they clattered over the bridge Pascent ran in front of them waving them down with his good arm.

'What brings you back so soon?'

'News that could not wait,' said Owain. 'We found a messenger with a half-spent horse in the Vale of Eddain. He was bringing word that men from Deur are crossing the Pennuin by the pass of Catraeth.'

'They're a bit late to burn the harvest.'

'It's no war band. They are coming to ask us for refuge. The kingdom of Deur has fallen to the Eingl of Bernicia.'

6

Myrddin's Brigantia

The next morning Urien sent a rider down the southern road to summon Llywarch from Caer Legion. Two days later the refugees from Deur arrived in Caer Lugualid; thirty horsemen with five mule carts holding their women and children, led by a stocky young man who introduced himself as Cugaun the last prince of the royal house of Deur.

Pascent passed on to me later the story Cugaun told Urien. He told how the kings of Deur had for years been holding off Eingl who had taken the flat coastlands of their southern frontier, but how in the last two summers they had come under attack from the north — from what had been Bryneich and was now Bernicia. It had ended in the month of the hazel when the two kings of Caer Ebrauc had fallen in battle, fighting a war band of Bernicians led by a king called Adda. Caer Ebrauc had been left almost undefended, and it had been the Eingl of southern Deur who had swept in to give the final blow to what had always seemed the strongest kingdom of northern Britain.

I could only whistle in amazement as the tale ended. 'What did your father say to that?' I asked Pascent.

'He was wonderful. He simply said he was sorry to hear of their misfortune and that they would be welcome to settle in some of the steadings in the forest which had lain empty since the men of Deur came cattle-raiding here three summers ago. You could see Cugaun squirming with shame.' Pascent stopped smiling. 'Otherwise my father has been keeping his thoughts to himself, but I think he's quite disturbed by the news. My bet is that he is waiting for Llywarch to get here and then he'll hold a council.'

'How I would love to be there when that happens,' I murmured.

'I was thinking the same thing,' said Pascent, 'and I think I know how we could be.'

Llywarch arrived two mornings later, and early that afternoon Pascent came to the smithy and persuaded Cialgrin that as he had made the sword which cut open Pascent's arm he could right the wrong by setting me free for the rest of the day. No sooner

43

were we both outside than Pascent began to walk as quickly as possible towards the centre of the city.

'I heard at midday,' he said, 'that my father is holding a small council this afternoon in the courtyard of the fountain. I think there will only be Llywarch, Myrddin and Owain with him.'

'How do we get in?' I asked.

'We don't,' he grinned. 'Remember how we saw from the walls that an empty garden backs onto the courtyard of the fountain? Well, I've explored it since, with Cairenn, and there is a bench where we can sit and hear everything that is said on the other side of the wall. You ought to hide there one day when you know Branwen is alone on the other side and play your harp very softly.'

We passed through the dark corridors of an empty house and tiptoed into a garden over heaps of fallen plaster and tangles of weeds. Sure enough, we could hear the voices on the far side of the wall even before we had reached the bench, onto which we lowered ourselves, hardly daring to breathe. I closed my eyes to hear better. The first voice I heard was the king's.

'Everything about the Eingl of Bernicia worries me,' he was saying. 'A few moons ago we routed a whole war band of theirs and yet they had the strength to cut down the kings of Deur in the same summer.'

'Surely Deur will give them all they want,' said Llywarch. 'It is a far richer land than Rheged.'

'Do you believe it will end there?' asked Urien. 'Three summers ago they took Bryneich and now they have taken Deur. It is my fear that three summers from now they will be wanting to take Rheged.'

'We have the mountains of Pennuin between us and Deur, and also the kingdom of Dunaut. He is still lord of the heart of old Brigantia.'

'And no friend of ours,' cut in Owain. 'He cannot be trusted to protect his own children. He would quite happily offer his services to the Eingl as a guide through the passes. . . .'

'And you forget, Llywarch,' said Urien, 'that they have already shown they are willing to cross the Pennuin by far wilder ways than the pass of Catraeth. We stopped them, but the ones we killed will have left kinsmen who will be just as willing to come over looking for vengeance.'

There was a silence, during which I glanced at Pascent. He looked pale, as pale as I would have looked if I had heard my father speak so openly with Outigern on the morning the Eingl burned Dun Guayrdi. The talking resumed in the courtyard of the fountain, and I heard Llywarch's voice.

'Then how do you suggest we meet this threat?'

'That, my cousin,' said Urien, 'is why I called you here. I hoped that you, with your age and experience, would be able to tell me.'

Llywarch burst out laughing. 'You always did have a honeyed tongue, Urien. You should have been a harper.'

'I begin to wish I had been. My thinking is this: we have to strike them before they strike us, while they are still busy picking the carcass of Deur. If we don't, and Bernicia and Deur are left free to grow into a kingdom larger and stronger than Rheged . . . well, it would not even help me to be a harper as there would be nothing left to sing about. We must throw them into the sea or before we are much older they will throw us into the sea.'

'It does seem,' said Llywarch, 'that the only choice we have is where, when, and how we die.'

'Perhaps,' said Urien.

'Not at all,' said Myrddin.

There was a stunned silence and I could imagine them all turning to stare at Myrddin.

'There is another way of seeing it,' he said. 'It can be looked at, as we have just done, as the problem of how to stop a wave from reaching the shore. It can also be looked at as the chance to destroy forever the power that set that wave in motion.'

'You get perilously close to riddles,' warned Urien.

'What I mean is this. We have spent our lifetime turning our eyes away from the growing strength of the Eingl on the east coast of Britain. We have had to, because most summers have brought war trails against our neighbours. We are even guilty of wishing the Eingl would turn on Deur because it was our enemy. We never remembered that we are all brothers, and because we forgot the real enemy grew strong and fed on our quarrels. . . .'

'Where is the hope in this?' groaned Urien.

'Now I will truly ask you a riddle,' said Myrddin. 'How did the Romans rule the north of Britain?'

'As one province,' said Llywarch.

'Correct. One province called Brigantia, from Caer Ebrauc in the east to Caer Lugualid in the west, from Caer Legion in the south to the Wall's end on the north-east coast. And what happened to Brigantia when Rome fell to pieces?'

'It became the kingdom of Coel Hen,' said Llywarch, 'and at

his death it was divided by his three sons.'

'Exactly, and over the years the separate kingdoms forgot their common root and took to war with each other, and that is why now Rheged stands all but alone.'

'I still do not see what is good in this,' said Urien.

'Because, Urien ap Cynvarch,' said Myrddin, his voice rising as though he were reaching the climax of a song, 'now that Deur has fallen and Bryneich has vanished, for the first time in three generations there is no war between the Britons of the north. If you succeed in crushing the Eingl the ground will be clear for you to once more make the north into one strong kingdom from sea to sea. That is what I mean when I say there are two ways of seeing Rheged. You can see it as the last kingdom of the old north, doomed to fall — if not in a few summers, at least within our lifetime — or you can see it as the first kingdom of a new north that will last for centuries and still be young in the days of Owain's children's children.'

'A fine vision,' said Urien softly. 'How would you set about it?'

'Och,' laughed Myrddin, his voice returning to normal. 'I give you a harper's vision of the end of a war. I'll leave the fighting of it to the warriors.'

'I can see a way to do it,' said Owain. 'If we took Catraeth we would command the passes to Rheged and drive a wedge between Bernicia and Deur. Between Deur and Rheged there is at least Dunaut for the little he is worth, so if we then moved against Bernicia. . . .'

'Which is also the Eingl's northern-most kingdom in Britain and the best place to begin,' agreed Urien.

'You see,' said Myrddin, 'with warriors like you it is possible.'

'I think I agree that it might be done,' said Llywarch, 'but not that it would bring peace to the north. We have not the legions with which the Romans ruled Brigantia. While it is true that our old enemies have fallen, in making ourselves masters of the north we could well make new ones. I cannot see Riderch of Strathclud loving us quite so much if we put his own power into shadow, and if we were to stretch our forces over three kingdoms I can see Gwynedd and Powys feeling free to let the old sores open.'

'True,' said Urien. 'The answer is to get Riderch to ride with us in this in return for the kingship of a new Bryneich. He is something of a Christian these days, he has monks where I have Myrddin, and I can imagine him liking the idea of a war trail against the pagans if he knew he were not going to ride alone. If he joined us we would be able to leave a war band in Caer Legion to remind the kings of Gwynedd and Powys where their hunting runs end and Rheged begins.'

'It begins to fall short of Myrddin's vision,' said Owain.

'It is still enough of a vision for me,' said Myrddin. 'To see Deur and Bryneich free again, to have in return a strong Rheged with no threat of the Eingl pouring over the Pennuin one fine summer . . . that would give me much to sing about.'

'And after all, it is that or darkness,' said Urien. 'We must make our plans for the spring, but we've talked enough for one day. Owain, find us some mead.'

Pascent nudged me and we tiptoed back across the deserted garden. Once we were in the streets we began to wander towards the ramparts. Neither of us could think of anything to say.

Urien made no public statement of his plans, but as the sad soft Rheged autumn gave way to a wet winter, Pascent and I found signs enough to interpret according to what we had overheard. My uncle and I found ourselves busier than usual at the smithy, the king having commissioned not only many spear and arrowheads but having also given us two cakes of pale Eriu gold which he wanted refashioned into bracelets of a set weight. Myrddin meanwhile became quite vexing. He had never been the easiest of teachers to understand or to keep up with, but now his wild moods swung unpredictably between days when he seemed to have forgotten I was training to be a harper and days when he wanted to cram a wealth of knowledge into me in a single afternoon, as though he had only a few days left to live.

The clearest sign of what was under way came with the two royal visitors Urien welcomed to Caer Lugualid in the last weeks of the year. The month of the reed brought Riderch of Strathclud, the oldest reigning king of the north. He looked as many as fifteen summers older than Urien, older even than Llywarch and Myrddin, and though his eyes had lost their brightness they were still quick to dart from side to side and take in all that happened around him. He and Urien hunted together, Owain riding beside Riderch's son Rioc, and there was much laughter and easy friendship in the feast-hall during their visit.

The second visitor, who came in the month of the elder as the year drew its last breath, left an unhappier taste in our mouths. This was Morcant Dhu, king of Manau Goddodin, nicknamed Morcant Sron because of the enormous nose which it was hard not to stare at. He was far younger than Urien, perhaps only some seven summers older than Owain, and he swaggered around Caer Lugualid with a jutting arrogance which endeared him to no-one. He brought with him a harper named Caw who when he was given the chance to sing sang of nothing but Morcant's courage, generosity and heroism. Pascent and I found it hard not to laugh, as to our knowledge Morcant had spent his life stealing cattle and doing little else, but Myrddin was appalled, saying that he used phrases reserved for the elegies of dead kings and that it was an insult both to harpers and to Urien.

Urien looked relieved when we reached the last evening of Morcant's visit, and seemed to be aching for the meal to end so that Myrddin's harping would free him from having to talk to the men who sprawled beside him in the place of honour where Riderch had sat with such dignity. Branwen was waiting on the high table, and I watched Morcant's turnip-coloured eyes gulping her in as she moved along with the mead-bowl. When she was opposite Morcant he turned sideways and placed his arm on Urien's arm.

'You would be truly inspired,' he began in a voice as over-pronounced as his harper's, 'if you saw fit to draw our two kingdoms closer together by offering me your fair daughter to be my bride.'

There was an immediate silence at the high table. Myrddin looked as though he would happily murder Morcant there and then, Urien's face became as impassive as a standing stone — always a bad sign — and Branwen's face was a bowl in which horror and disgust had been mixed to turn her as pale as the moon. I all but suffered a bout of the breathing sickness as I realised the pressure Morcant was placing on Urien by asking him in front of the whole feast-hall, for it gave Urien no way of refusing without casting a public slur on Morcant's honour. Urien glanced at Branwen, reading the signs of revulsion in her face, then drew a deep breath and turned back to his guest.

'You do my daughter great honour with your desire. You know that the great sadness of my life is that I have no queen; she died in giving birth to Branwen. Because of that my daughter has long promised me that she will wait on me in her mother's place and be no man's bride until I myself have gone beyond the sunset to rejoin the woman I love. I thank you again for your offer Morcant, but I regret that it can never come to pass as long as I live.'

Morcant's mouth opened, as though to reply, then flapped shut again. An almost audible breath of relief swept through all

48

the men of Rheged around the high table. We knew Urien was lying, but even if Morcant did too there was no way for him to make that accusation to the king's face. Branwen returned to the cooking fires where she sat very still and Urien broke the silence by clapping the palm of his hand on the table.

'Myrddin! A song for our royal guest!'

Myrddin rose to the occasion by telling the tale of Bricriu's feast: how Bricriu held a banquet for the warriors of Ulster and tried to make them quarrel, and how the warriors of Ulster repaid him by tearing the house down.

The following morning the clouds were low and a fine drizzle chilled everyone as Morcant took his leave of Urien in the square of Caer Lugualid. Owain was to ride with Morcant as far as the border of Strathclud, which lay between Rheged and Manau Goddodin. As the horsemen clattered down the cobbles of the street leading to the north gate, Myrddin spat noisily into the square.

'It is in my thoughts we should be fighting them, not trying to make them our friends.'

Urien half-smiled, pausing in the doorway of the hall to shake the drizzle from his green woollen cloak. 'Be careful what you say or it may come to that. It does seem a sad thing to spill our blood riding to free Bryneich if it means carrion like them will once more have the freedom of her hunting trails.'

'Still, we ride for Brigantia, not for them,' said Myrddin.

'Aye,' said Urien, 'and to give you something to sing about in your old age. Whatever we ride for, we won't let worms like that stand in our way.'

7

The Plain of Deur

The winter ended with snow, but quite gently, and the spring brought many new lambs and calves. The feast of Beltane came as the moon was waning, and it was then, as the fires burned low and the last of the dancers ran laughing in pairs towards the trees, that Urien sent out word for the war host to muster when the moon was next full.

Caer Lugualid became a hive; it could not have seen such activity since the days of the legions. I spent the mornings helping my uncle prepare all he needed for a field-forge which, with as many weapons as we had in stock, had to fit into two small mule carts. The afternoons I spent with Fionn, who taught me the use of her healing salves, for I was to ride with the war host as a healer as well as a harper. I was slower with this new craft than I was with the learning of songs, but she repeated her teaching with infinite patience. Perhaps she thought that it might come down to me to ensure that Cialgrin returned alive to her and little Dichuil.

By the end of the month of the willow each day brought more warriors to Caer Lugualid, and the feast-hall became so crowded that finally it overflowed into the square. These were the men of Rheged and a good number of men from Deur, who had been crossing the Pennuin in Cugaun's wake throughout the winter. I had heard from Pascent that Riderch of Strathclud would join us later, when we reached the borders of Bryneich.

When we reached the borders of Bryneich . . . the very words made my head sing. I had only to wander through the gathered warriors and hear Myrddin singing the old hunting songs to imagine myself riding in triumph through the gateway of Caer Brighid. For four winters my uncle had been the loneliest man I knew, keeping himself to the forge and to Fionn and little Dichuil, but now he sat among the warriors with a light in his eyes which did not come from the mead. Pascent understood how we were feeling. We looked at the host that had gathered and had not a moment's doubt of our success.

The one man who seemed to stand apart from it all was Urien himself. He made the warriors welcome, he was everywhere seeing to the preparations, but he had not the spring in his step which could be seen in Owain's. I found out why, and saw it change, on the afternoon before the moon came to fullness.

Urien came to the smithy to see that my uncle and I had made ready the mule carts. He was standing talking to Cialgrin about spear-shafts when a figure walked down the street behind him. He looked some two summers younger than Owain and wore the simple clothes of a monk. A quiet smile played on his lips as he stopped behind the king.

'Father,' he said.

Urien spun round. A door seemed to open in his face, then slam shut again. 'Elphin,' he said. 'What brings you here?'

'The word is that you are riding against the Eingl.'

'So, will you pray for me in the hovels of your monastery?' Urien's voice was cold, and a flicker of a blush coloured the young man's face. He pushed it down and fixed his father with eyes of grey-brown, a mixture of Owain's and Branwen's. I wondered what bitter words had passed between them in the past to make their meeting so strained. Elphin's reply was slow and clear.

'If you ride against the Eingl you are not riding for land or cattle, you are riding against the darkness of the pagans. I want to come with you.'

Urien's shoulders seemed to slump, then he opened his arms and moved forward to bury his head on Elphin's shoulder. 'I do thank God for this,' he said. 'Forgive me.'

'There's nothing to forgive, father,' said Elphin. They stood clasped together, and my uncle and I went softly into the smithy.

The following morning the war host rode out of Caer Lugualid with Urien at the head in red and green which matched the colours of the Dragon banner of Rheged. There were more warriors than I had ever seen; Urien had mustered some five hundred horsemen, and Cugaun added to that four score horsemen of Deur. Behind the riders came the long column of pack ponies and mule carts. The stones of the Roman road rang beneath the horses' hooves as though singing their own song of gladness at once more having a legion to travel them.

All day we rode south, taking our time because it was senseless to push the horses when they would have to carry us twice the width of Britain and more. To our west the peaks of the Lake Mountains rose into the sky, still streaked with white ribs of snow, and to our east we could see the more sombrely rolling mountains of Pennuin into which we would ride on the morrow.

By the end of the afternoon we had reached the crossroads where we were to take the eastern road, and there we made camp for the night in a ruined rath. The men of Rheged had none of the sense of Roman ghosts which had filled me on my journey out of Bryneich with my uncle, perhaps because they lived in a town so full of them. They moved around happily, settling the horses and making cooking fires of furze root and rotten timber. The evenings were growing longer so it was not until well after we had eaten our broiled mutton, rye bread and cheese that I was called upon to sing. I played my harp by the king's fire while Myrddin and Llywarch moved from fire to fire amongst the host.

In the morning we took the eastern road which led up the Vale of Eddain. It was rich cattle country and Pascent joked that Cugaun and the men of Deur must know it all too well from their misdeeds in the past. It was a beautiful day, the pale greens and yellows of spring were in the new leaves of the trees, and we made camp that night in the Roman rath at the head of the valley. The men of Eddain had used it as a cattle pen since the Romans left and we had to be careful where we unrolled our sleeping blankets.

The next morning the road led up into the high valley of the Eddain. The oak and alder scrub gave place to odd clumps of stunted hazel and rowan, and we entered a landscape of heather and moor-grass broken only by empty bothies waiting for the shepherds to bring their flocks up to the summer pastures. Late in the morning we reached the height of the pass where a standing stone marked the borders of Rheged and Deur. Urien stopped the column and invited Cugaun and his men to ride with him at the head. Pascent and I found ourselves pushed well back from where the Elphin rode with the banner.

'Such courtesy,' laughed Pascent. 'It must be in my father's mind that if Dunaut is lying in wait for us somewhere it may as well be Cugaun who gets an arrow in the throat.'

'Do you think he will be?' I asked.

'Not him, he'll be skulking in the wide valleys well south of here. I wish he would attack, then we could kill two boars in the same hunting.'

Nonetheless, I could see Pascent keeping his eyes on the skyline of the hills which rose on either side of us. I had none of his fears. I was too taken up with a wild exhilaration, and too busy trying to imagine what had brought it on. I knew it was not the riding; it was four winters since I had been in the saddle for three days in a row and I ached in every bone. Then I realised that I was drinking the air and that what excited me was the rush of high streams, the patches of fresh green bracken on the hillsides, and the song of the curlew. It was simply that I had been born among hills, spent my childhood among them, and it was good to be back.

By the middle of the afternoon the highest of the hills were behind us and we were coming down the high valley of the Tees, which widened out ahead of us towards a forested plain which formed our eastern horizon. Beyond that must be the sea. We made our halt just above the Tees where a Roman rath lay in a small valley with a swift stream. The men of Rheged made their cooking fires in a circle, for they were no longer in their own lands. The men of Deur set their fires by the stream. Messengers arrived for the Cugaun and we watched him receive them.

'All hail the prince returned from exile,' muttered Pascent. 'I suppose he's telling them we offered him our services.'

I was playing the harp by the king's fire later that evening when Cugaun's stocky figure appeared on the outer edge of the firelight.

'My lord Urien,' he said, clapping his hands together like someone who has just won a horse race.

'Welcome, my lord Cugaun. Join us and tell us your news.'

He squatted down on the opposite side of the fire to the king. I laid my harp across my knees and watched the firelight playing on the faces of Urien, Owain and Elphin as they waited for him to speak.

'I have made arrangements for warriors to join us and for a food tribute to be collected for us,' he began. 'I have also received enough news to form a picture of Deur. . . .'

'He'll need one if he's ever going to be its king,' whispered Pascent.

'The armies that crushed my father and uncle have returned to Bernicia but are expected to come back later this spring. Caer Ebrauc is in the hands of Eingl from the south, who will soon hear of our coming and are likely to march against us at once. They are strong but they are the only force who stand in our way at present. It is in my mind that if we struck fast at Caer Ebrauc we could be masters of Deur within a week.'

Cugaun sat beaming enthusiasm and waiting for Urien's reply. It was hard not to like him, and he had at least said 'we'. Urien nodded and for a few moments seemed to be drawing with his finger in the soil at his feet, then he looked up and fixed Cugaun with his grey gaze.

'It is all good news but it worries me to have the war host of Bernicia somewhere out of sight to our north. Our plan was to secure Catraeth, cut the north-south road and keep the Eingl of Deur locked in the south while we ride north to take Bernicia. If we press south now there is always the chance the Bernicians might race down and catch us south of Catraeth. I prefer that for now we go only to Catraeth and meet whoever comes against us there.'

Cugaun slapped his knees and rose to his feet. 'I can see the wisdom in that,' he sighed.

'Tomorrow Catraeth,' said Urien, 'and Deur by the autumn.'

As we broke camp in the dawnlight there were pools of mist in the lowest parts of the plain of the Tees while high above us a flat curtain of cloud had been drawn across the sky. It made me think of the Eingl to our south and the Eingl to our north, and it was good to be riding with men who did not have a harper's imagination. Pascent groaned as he heaved himself into the saddle.

'This Catraeth,' he said. 'It's on the road so it must be Roman, eh?'

'I think so. Myrddin said he once went there. It's about half the size of Caer Lugualid.'

Pascent sighed happily. 'You know what that means?'

'No.'

'It means level floors to sleep on. What are we waiting for?'

Our ride took us along the edge of the plain of the Tees in a south-easterly direction, keeping the edge of the Pennuin to our right. We were riding through forests again, and we rode as quickly as the mule carts could manage, all too aware that we could be ambushed in the same way as we had ambushed the Bernicians by the Lleven. But the trees hid no warriors and in the late morning we crested a low hillock to see the north-south road running across our path, with nothing but low shrubs for a spear's throw on either side where the Romans had cut back the trees. Our way lay south, through the same landscape mile after mile until in mid-afternoon we rode through wasted fields to a wide river and saw on the other side the rotting ramparts of Catraeth, with not a single spume of hearth-smoke rising upwards from within.

Entering it was strange. No soldier's rath this, but a town like Caer Lugualid, only dead. As we rode through a pattern of streets like a small mirror of Urien's capital I had a vision of what the leaving of the Romans had meant. They must have built Catraeth because of the road, one of a chain of towns throughout Britain in the days when the roads were travelled by many. Once they had gone the traders vanished, the traffic dwindled, and it became an obvious target for raiders; it must have suffered them until the last townspeople took to the forest or the hills. It made me imagine what Caer Lugualid would become without Urien.

We spent the rest of the day trying to clear ourselves sleeping places among the ghosts. Our previous camps had been in raths long abandoned, their buildings nothing but overgrown shells; now we moved among standing houses with old doors that fell from their hinges when pushed open. Pascent sat on a cross-legged chair which immediately splintered and collapsed. The old basilica in the main square was falling apart at the north end, but Urien and Cugaun set men to clear the rest of the building to make a feast-hall. By evening it had at last been brought back to life, and the whole host gathered to eat while the firelight sent shadows dancing up the bare and mouldy walls. There was still a deep sadness about Catraeth which shortened our laughter and made it hard to think of a good song to sing.

It was late before the men drifted away in groups to sleep among the dead houses. I was grateful to have my harper's place by the king's fire. Pascent fell asleep quickly, but the strangeness of the place kept me awake. After much tossing and turning I sat up and looked about the hall, and my eyes made out the figure of Myrddin sitting by the dull glow of one of the fires. I wrapped my cloak around me and made my way over the sleeping warriors to join him. As I sat down beside him he acknowledged me with a nod and went back to staring into the embers.

After a while I broke the silence. 'What happens now?' I asked.

'Now?' he replied slowly. 'Now we wait, and hope the Eingl are not long in coming. It is easy to get a war host to ride, but hard to make it sit still and wait for its prey to show.'

'You sound almost sad.'

'I am sad tonight.' He looked around the bare walls. 'I was here many years ago when I was even younger than you are now. It was still a busy town then, and a proud one. There were men who remembered seeing Artos ride north, proud men. They used to say that the Sea Wolves could eat up Britain but that Catraeth would be the last town to fall.'

'Then we will avenge them.'

'Mmmm. . . . All I know is the width of the chasm between Catraeth of my memory and this dead place. When we left Caer Lugualid I was dreaming of the Brigantia we were riding to save . . . now we are here I find it has not waited for us to come.'

'Surely,' I said, 'if we are here, the dream is alive, and as long as we ride, the dream lives?'

'Perhaps, but dreams are private things and tonight I can only stare into the embers of mine.' He turned to look into my eyes. 'What is it you dream of, Gwion ap Talhearn my pupil?'

It was my turn to look into the fire. 'I dream of being as good a harper as my father, and that we will free Bryneich so I can one day sing where he sang in the hall of Caer Brighid.'

'You will be the harper your father was,' said Myrddin. 'As to the rest, I hope it comes to you. Perhaps our dreams are simply the measure of all we have lost.' He reached out and laid a hand on my shoulder. 'Sleep now, little Gwion, and may your dreams take you home.'

Myrddin was right about how the war host would find it hard to sit still. The next day brought rain and a score of riders who wished to fight beside Cugaun, but it brought no news of the Eingl of Caer Ebrauc. By the following day the men of Rheged were beginning to kick their heels and grumble. It was one thing to ride to defend one's own land or even to cross the border for a quick cattle-raid or battle, but quite another to be told to sit in a rotting town in another country listening to the rain dripping through the holes in the roofs. There were two minor quarrels which nearly became fights, so on our third morning in Catraeth Urien allowed some of the men to ride out hunting and ordered the rest to do what they could to repair the walls of the town.

In the afternoon I invoked my role as my uncle's helper and went and sat in the room he had adapted into a smithy. He was out somewhere and there was no sound to be heard except the rain, which ended by lulling me to sleep. I was woken by shouts and the sound of running feet splashing down the street, and by the time I reached the doorway the street was crowded with men saddling their horses and gathering their weapons. I made out the face of Fracan, one of Urien's companions, and dodged through the horses till I was as close to him as I could get without being trampled.

'What's happening?' I yelled.

'Eingl on the road from Caer Ebrauc,' he called back. 'They're only about three miles away.'

The words sank into my sleep-slurred mind. Three miles meant that they would only be a matter of minutes distant. I spun round and headed for the square where my horse Faencha was stabled, progressing in hops and slithers along the wet street while warriors clattered past on their horses. The square was a seething mass of riders and twice I came close to being crushed as I squeezed my way through the centre of the press. Luckily I made out the red tuft of Pascent's hair and saw that he had Faencha beside him, already saddled.

'Where were you?' he asked as I hauled myself into the saddle.

'Asleep,' I gasped.

'Dreaming of Branwen again?'

I had no time to reply as Urien had ordered the horns to be blown and we were riding towards the south gate of the town. Once through it we fanned out across the road and the low-shrubbed verges on either side and began to gallop. The Red Dragon banner fluttered in the centre of the road, but otherwise the men of Rheged and Deur were mixed together in one body of horsemen, gathering speed and screaming war cries into the rain. The braying of our horns was echoed by a deeper booming of war horns further down the road, causing us to yell and urge our horses to go faster. I felt the sickness of fear turn my stomach to nothingness.

All at once the air hummed and a flight of arrows was among us. A rider to my left took one in the chest and the next instant the horse beside me was riderless, but we were moving too fast and in too tight a pack to make it even worth turning to try and see where he had fallen. The yelling ahead grew louder, and with numb co-ordination I took the reins in my left hand and drew my dirk. The horses ahead of us lurched as though hit by a wave, then surged forward again, and I knew we had met our enemy. The air filled with shouts, screams and the clash of weapons; it even seemed that the rain beat down harder.

Then we were among the Eingl, our charge breaking round groups of them like a stream breaks round boulders. I caught glimpses of faces set in the snarls of battle but I kept my eyes on their weapons, for they were laying about with axes which could cut my horse from under me and if that happened I would be dead. I found myself wedged between Pascent on my right and a companion of Llywarch's named Gwedian on my left who

57

between them carved a wake through the Eingl which I had only to follow, which was just as well, for it was all I could do to stay in the saddle as Faencha kicked his way over bushes and fallen men.

We broke through the far side of the Eingl war host, and we knew then that we had overpowered them, so it was with shouts of victory that we turned and rode back for the kill. I saw the chaos of the battle straddling the road, the Eingl forming into clusters and our riders bearing down on them to break them apart, the individual struggles moving in different directions over ground littered with fallen men and traversed by riderless horses. I knew I could be no use in the fight, so when Pascent and Gwedian turned to join the harrying of one group of Eingl I aimed Faencha straight down the road and came out shaking and shivering on the Catraeth side of the battle.

I rode back to the men who had fallen from the arrow flight. They were all dead, trampled by our own horses and twisted into weird broken-limbed positions, soaked by the rain and spattered with mud looking as though they had been dead a day and not a handful of minutes. I slid from my saddle, dropped to the ground and began retching up the contents of my stomach onto the grass.

When at last I stood up and turned towards the fight I saw a Rheged man staggering out of the chaos with blood running from a gash in his side. I ran towards him and made him lie down while I cut a strip from the cloak of one of the dead and set about binding the wound as tightly as possible. I looked up to see that the battle had broken into a series of running fights moving down the road towards Caer Ebrauc, and while Urien and his warriors drove the Eingl to flight and cut them down as they ran, I moved among the fallen doing what I could for wounds which would have turned my stomach if I had had any stomach left to turn.

I was too exhausted to sing that evening, but Llywarch was in fine voice so it hardly mattered. While the battle had been raging on the south road, men of Deur had ridden in at the north gate with several carts of food, including a good quantity of heather beer which it was evident would not outlive the evening. The fires were piled high and our soaked garments steamed on our backs. Pascent lay stretched out beside me, his fingers playing over a mail-shirt he had taken from among the Eingl dead with the same joy with which mine usually played over my harp strings.

'If Owain does not watch himself,' he said, 'we'll have a new suitor for Branwen my father might find it harder to refuse.' I looked over to where Owain and Cugaun were sitting arm in arm. The story that was on everyone's lips was how Owain and Geraint had found themselves surrounded by a group of Eingl, and how they would have been cut down had Cugaun not seen them and ridden over with help. Now they sat like the oldest of brothers in arms, talking, with the help of the heather beer, of how before autumn came they would ride together into Caer Ebrauc.

Myrddin was making his way through the crowd, weary after hours spent tending the wounded. His eyes, normally alive with their own wild light, were blank. An impulse took hold of me and I went over to him.

'Look at Owain and Cugaun,' I said. 'The dream does live for them. There can still be a new Brigantia.'

8

Hollow Hills

Seven evenings later I saw the Wall again. We had taken the road north from Catraeth, leaving Cugaun and the men of Deur to hold it till our return, and four days of riding had brought us in one straight line to the very rath my uncle and I had passed through on our flight to Rheged. It was very different now. As we crossed the moor towards it we could see the smoke of many cooking fires, and warriors on the ramparts, for it was the night of the new moon and Riderch of Strathclud had brought his war host south to meet us.

He greeted us inside the gateway, flanked by Rioc his son and a royal-looking man with a crest of fair hair and a tunic richly embroidered in spiral patterns. Urien swung down from the saddle and he and Riderch embraced amidst a clamour of cheering.

'You come as we planned, and I am here as we planned,' said Riderch. He called forward the fair-haired man. 'I bring with me Echu Mac Luin, a chief among the men of Dalriada on my nothern border. I told him of our hunting trail and he has brought a hundred spears to join it.'

'Then he is doubly welcome,' said Urien.

There was much to do to make ready for the night. With the men of Strathclud and Dalriada we were now a host of twelve hundred, and being the last arrivals the men of Rheged found themselves making camp on the bare moor outside the rath. By good luck it was a soft night, and there was no shortage of supple young bracken with which to bed out the hollows of the moor. We ate in the rath, feasting on roasted lamb and goat, and there was so much singing that we were well into the darkness before the conversation by the fire of the kings turned to the reason of our meeting.

'For the first two days of the journey north our outriders found several villages of Eingl,' said Urien, 'but these last two days we have found them deserted. Word of our coming must be spreading fast, and I should judge they will be massing for battle before the moon is much older.'

'We came by way of the hills,' said Riderch, 'so we have no news either of Bryneich or of the Wolves that infest it. We do know they have their royal seat at Dun Guayrdi on the coast, and it will be there they will muster their war host.'

'Then it is there we shall go,' said Urien.

'The legions have left us a road,' said Riderch. 'It branches towards the coast a few miles north of the Wall. We can be there in three days at the most.'

'There seems little left for us to decide.' Urien looked around the fire. 'What has become of Morcant of Manau Goddodin? I thought he would be here to ride with us.'

'He sent word that he will cross the Tuid when he hears we have reached Dun Guayrdi,' replied Riderch. Rioc his son made a wry expression and spat noisily into the fire.

'So,' laughed Urien, 'those of us who are to ride together are all here. Let us ride on tomorrow.'

'You would not rest your men?'

'We rested in Catraeth, and it is a place to make men hate having to rest. No, we ride on now to Dun Guayrdi, and rest when we have driven the Eingl into the sea. There is much to do this summer.'

I slipped away from the fires to wander to the ramparts of the rath, and found a place where holes left by a rotted wooden stairway enabled me to climb onto the Wall. I stood for a moment looking down on the crowded rath and the circles of warriors gathered around the fires, then turned to the north and looked out at the dark shapes of the hills under the night sky. They were the hills of Bryneich, and they were calling to me, sending feelings without name to catch my breath and set me shivering despite the softness of the night.

Beyond the horizon lay Caer Brighid, where there must still be some people gathered round the old hearth fires if the Eingl had left them alone and kept to Dun Guayrdi. I wanted to be there, and I knew from what I had just heard that the war host would take the coast road and see Caer Brighid only as a hill on their western skyline as they neared Dun Guayrdi. It was somehow wrong that whoever might still cling to Outigern's rath should have no part in the freeing of Bryneich. I tore my eyes away from the dark hills, lowered myself from the rampart and jumped to the ground. I ran back to the fires possessed by an idea.

Myrddin looked up at me as I re-entered the firelight. 'What is it? You look as if you've seen the White Hag herself.'

'Not that,' I said, 'but I have seen something else. It is wrong that we ride into Bryneich without sending word to any who might still be living in the rath of King Outigern.'

'Wrong?' said Urien, with much the same look he had given me the summer before when I had refused to remain in Caer Lugualid with the women.

Riderch ran his hand abstractly round the ancient gold torc which was clasped around his neck. 'Outigern has been dead four summers. He left no sons.'

I talked on blindly. 'Still we should send word to his old hearth of what we are to do if we want his spirit, the spirit of Bryneich, to be with us when we go into battle.'

Urien nodded. 'How would you have us do this, Gwion my harper?'

'Let me ride there, by the hill roads I travelled four autumns ago. I can be there in two days, and if there are any warriors I can bring them to you four days from now at Dun Guayrdi. If there are not, then I will sing of us to the ghosts so they know who it is that takes over their hunting.'

'You have my leave to do this,' said Urien. 'Owain will see that you have a saddle-bag of food. The sun and the moon be on your path.'

I could not tell what the men around the fire thought of my wish, but they accepted it, telling themselves perhaps that I was after all only a harper and could not be expected to have a warrior's common sense. As soon as it was arranged I felt weary with relief, as though I had answered the call of the hills, and I was almost puzzled when Owain gave me a saddle-bag of barley bannock, cold roast lamb and stale nuts.

'My father told me to give you these,' he said, and handed me three of the bracelets Cialgrin had made from Urien's Eriu gold. 'Wear them on your left arm, high under your sleeve, and use them if you have need of them.' He looked at me with those grey eyes so like his father's. 'Gwion, what is all this about?'

'I don't know,' I replied, my strange eloquence having burnt itself out. 'It's just something I can feel calling me.'

'It could be the calling of his father's harp,' said Myrddin, 'or something between him and the hills. I have times when the forest calls to me; it is like that for him.'

Owain shook his head, slapped me on the shoulder and went off to his sleeping place. Myrddin stood looking down at me.

'I know you do not fear these hills,' he said, 'but do not trust them. At all times keep your eyes open, and if you come across strangers, melt into the hillside till you know who they are. Try not to lose your harp in some bog; it was long in the making.'

I hardly slept, and was grateful when dawn came and I could leave. I wove my way through the slowly stirring encampment and took Faencha from the picket. Only when I had ridden through the north gate of the rath and left the Wall behind did my heart stop thumping and relax. Ahead of me the road ran over empty hills, and I could hear nothing but the song of the birds and the gusting of the wind.

It came to me that I had no idea if I could really reach Caer Brighid in two days, and the first flicker of doubt was kindled in my mind. It was also the last time I was to have the loneliness for kindling, for I rode over a rise to see in a hollow a horse I knew and, stretched out on the heather, a figure I knew even better. Pascent sprang to his feet and had mounted before I drew level with him.

'I thought I'd wait for you here,' he said, scratching his head. 'What for?'

'So you can show me Bryneich as we ride.'

I knew before the morning was much older how grateful I was that Pascent had taken it into his head to come with me. After days of keeping to the pace of a war host with mule carts it was a joy to set our horses galloping and to feel the moor vibrate to a drumming of hooves which sent alarmed grouse hastily skyward from their nests in the heather. We urged each other on and by the middle of the afternoon had reached the Roman rath below which Cialgrin and I had camped. We rested the horses then pressed on, following the road over hills speckled with the gold flowers of gorse, and towards evening came down into the high valley where the skeleton of a rath was overgrown with bracken and lush moor-grass. We scraped together the gorse roots and old heather twigs to give us a fire, loosed the horses to graze, and by nightfall were wrapped in our cloaks and feasting on cold meat and barley bannock.

In the morning the road took us to the crest of the next hills, down which it stretched away into the high valley of the Tuid. Our way, however, turned to the west along the old Votadini trackway which followed the ridges to Yr Cerrid, whose brooding bulk I could now see in the eastern skyline. We set our horses along the ridge, looking down at the streams and valleys which fell away to either side, feeling ourselves to be following the very spine of the hills. By late afternoon we were crossing the flat top of Yr Cerrid, and finally we reached the moment I had longed for. The view eastward opened up beneath us, the hills rolling in ever-lower waves to where Caer Brighid looked out over wooded valleys to the sea beyond. I pointed it out to Pascent and he grinned back.

'It's worth fighting for, this land of Bryneich.'

We rode on, losing height so that our view was once more of the hills around us and their immediate valleys, until, with the horses nearly spent, we drew rein on the high shoulder below the twin-breasted summit of Caer Brighid. Looking up at the rath in the mellow haze of evening we could see no moving figures, and only one column of bluish peak smoke rising into the sky. We dismounted to lead the horses up the last steep slope to the gateway, and I noticed that the track was overgrown, as though few feet and no horses had climbed the hill in the last few winters. Clusters of yellow and blue star-shaped flowers grew where in my childhood Outigern's horses had left only a streak of bare earth, and as we drew level with the gateway we found ourselves walking on a carpet of clumps of grass.

There were no horses to be seen in the rath. We tethered ours by the gateway and made our way into the feast-hall. It was empty and lifeless, there was no trace of the smells I remembered from childhood, and it had evidently not seen use in a long time. There were holes in the thatching of the roof and one of the embroidered wall-hangings lay crumpled and rotting on the floor.

'Lord of Light!' muttered Pascent. 'I hope this never happens to Rheged.'

We went outside and round the corner in search of the bothy with a fire alight, startling two sheep who collided in their haste to get out of our path. I knew before we came to it that the bothy was my mother's. When we reached its low threshold we found the door-curtain drawn and could hear no sound from within but the hissing splutter of the burning peat. Pascent's hand tightened on his sword-hilt. I took a last look round at the deserted rath and then spoke in what I hoped was a steady voice.

'Mother? It's me, Gwion.'

There was a rustle of movement and the door-curtain was drawn back. My mother stepped out into the light, and I moved backwards at the shock of seeing her. Her hair had turned completely white and there was a stoop to her shoulders. My mouth hung open, and I realised from her eyes that she saw many changes in me. It was she who spoke, in the rich voice my father had always called the sweetest song he knew.

'Whatever brings you back here?' Her voice quickened with worry. 'Are the Sea Wolves chasing you?'

'Mother, you are the first face I've seen in Bryneich,' I mumbled.

She glanced at Pascent. 'And who is your companion?'

'Pascent ap Urien, of Rheged,' he replied with an awkward smile.

'Then you are both welcome,' she said simply. 'Come inside.'

'A blessing be upon this dwelling and on the lady of its hearth,' said Pascent as we ducked under the threshold, his words nearly stumbling on his lips at the sight which met our eyes. There were two other women crouching on the far side of the hearth. One of them was old and withered, and the second was my age and sat biting her fingernails and staring out at us from under a tangle of matted hair.

'You will remember Eorann and Emer,' said my mother.

'Of course. Greetings to you both,' I mumbled. The words we were speaking seemed hopelessly out of place. 'Tell me, are you three all who remain at Caer Brighid?'

'We have been these last two winters,' said my mother, offering Pascent a bowl of ewe's milk. 'The Wolves took many of us away. They left Eorann because of her age, me because I played blind, and Emer we had hidden. After a while they left us alone. They are not people of the hills, the Sea Wolves.'

'What of Uaran?'

'They took him to be a thrall in Dun Guayrdi, as they did with most of those they took away.' My mother spoke with an acceptance in her voice which hurt me more than what she said. 'You look well,' she said. 'Is the breathing sickness still with you?'

'No, it is gone.'

'And how is Cialgrin?'

'He is well. He has a wife and son. . . .' I found I was shaking my head as words failed me.

'Four winters ago he and his uncle arrived at my father's court in Caer Lugualid,' said Pascent. 'They have been with us ever since, Cialgrin as a smith and Gwion as a harper.'

A spark flickered in my mother's eyes. 'You are a harper?'

'I am the pupil of a harper named Myrddin. He once met father in Caer Ebrauc.'

For the first time she smiled. 'That is good. It is more than I dreamed.' Suddenly it was she who was lost for words. Her face creased as though she were swallowing pain. She gave a small wave of her hand as though to brush it away then looked into my eyes. 'My son, it has been hard living without knowing if you were alive or dead. If I seem cold it is that I have had to make myself forget you. So tell me, why do you come back now?'

'To bring great news. A day's ride behind us are the war hosts of Rheged and Strathclud. Before the moon is full we will have thrown the Wolves back into the sea and Bryneich will be free again. I have come to find any warriors who once rode with Outigern and to bid them join us in the battle.'

My mother groaned. 'Fools, why are all men such fools? There are none of Outigern's men left in Bryneich, and even if there were I would not tell you where to find them. I have spent my life watching men and their sons dying for this land, and if I have had one relief these last four winters it has been knowing that the fighting was over. If you have come back just so I may keen over your dead body then I wish you had stayed away.'

'It is true,' joined in old Eorann, 'there are no victories to be won here. If you win Bryneich the struggle will only begin again, and if you fail to win it the Wolves will burn out the last of us so that the land is all theirs. Go back to Rheged and look to your own hearths and harvests.'

All they said brought back to me my talk with Myrddin by the fire at Catraeth and left me speechless. It was Pascent who replied.

'We are here to protect our own hearths and harvests. Last summer the Eingl from this coast came over the hills to Rheged, and made a hunting trail to the south into Deur. We are taking up the fight your men lost because it has come to us and does not give us the choice of fighting or turning away, only of winning or losing.'

The women fell silent and Pascent continued.

'We ask you then for one night's hospitality before we ride to rejoin our companions.'

'It is yours,' said my mother. 'You know you are welcome, and you know our hearts will ride with you. Tonight we can only offer you the poorest of meals.'

'To us it will be a feast,' said Pascent. 'We have ridden far, and we must leave you now to tend to our horses.'

He clapped me on the shoulder and I rose numbly to follow him outside. The rath seemed golden in the twilight as we walked round to the door of the feast-hall to see the horses grazing calmly. Pascent gave a long low whistle and sat down with his back against the disused weapon-stone where once the men of the Votadini had sharpened their swords.

'So we are too late to save Bryneich, and all we can do is purge it,' he said.

'Let's take the horses and leave now,' I heard myself saying.

'I wish we could, but the horses are spent and I ache all over. This place is too much like the old tales of the hollow hills, not that I would feel much loss if we woke up tomorrow to find nothing but bare hilltop.'

After seeing to the horses we wandered aimlessly round the ramparts, which felt as dead as a rath of the Romans, and I pointed out the landmarks of Bryneich and the far hills of Manau Goddodin. We lingered until dusk closed in and the air grew cold, then made our way back to the bothy, whose light and warmth had become welcome.

Some of the strangeness passed during the meal. We added the last of our cold meat to the women's vegetable stew, and it was followed by the ewe's milk cheese flavoured with garlic which I remembered so well from my childhood. My mother asked many questions about life in Rheged, and when the meal was over I brought out my harp and sang a few of the songs I knew my father to have sung. The music did much to fill my emptiness, as it had so often before. The weariness from our journey crept upwards through our bones, and when sleep came it came easily and brought no bad dreams.

We took our leave early the next morning. I promised to return once the fighting was done and my mother gave us cheese, a fresh barley bannock and a small wooden pot of honey. I felt more at peace, as though some question within me had been answered, and the sun felt warm on our shoulders as we rode down the flanks of Caer Brighid into the wooden valley of the Glein.

It was out of place to feel so at peace when the most dangerous part of our journey lay before us. We had expected to meet no-one on the high hills, but here in the fertile valleys, the heartland of Eingl Bernicia, we ran every risk of riding into a settlement or a band of warriors. There was nothing we could do except ride with all speed for the coast road and hope that the first people we met were from Rheged or Strathclud.

We followed the beck of the Glein down to the river Till then took the track upstream, knowing only that the Roman road forded it well below its headwaters. We rode south-east, parallel to the coast which could not be many miles distant over the low hills to our left. Late in the morning we rode straight into the clearing of a farmstead, but it was deserted and we galloped across it with our hearts in our mouths but with no dogs barking or men running for weapons. Once we were back amongst the trees our spirits rose, as the emptiness suggested that Urien must be near.

Our luck ran out in the afternoon. The stream was narrower and running more rapidly when we turned eastwards towards the hills from which it sprang. We were riding along a stretch of bank where the tree cover was sparser when we heard a shout and turned to see horsemen on the top of a knoll some five spear-throws above us. They yelled and urged their horses down the slope towards us. Pascent and I took one look at each other and kicked our horses into a gallop.

I wrapped my hands in Faencha's mane and held on in terror while the trees on either side of us became a blur and my heart hammered harder than storm-rain on the tiles of Caer Lugualid. Faencha streaked after Pascent's horse while I shut my eyes and waited for a spear or a throwing-axe to hit me between the shoulder-blades. As soon as I felt used to the sickening speed I turned to look over my shoulder. Our pursuers were still a good way behind. I turned to look ahead only to receive a blow to the chest which lifted me out of the saddle and threw me to the ground.

For a moment I was conscious of nothing but pain and a buzzing in my ears as though my head had landed in a wasp's nest. Then I heard Faencha snorting and opened my eyes to see Pascent turning to ride back towards me. I could hear the hoofbeats of our pursuers closing on us as Pascent leapt from his saddle and blasted on the hunting horn he carried on his belt in a desperate attempt to make the Eingl believe we had friends nearby. They did not stop, and Pascent drew his sword and stood over me. I looked up to see the vibrating branch of a hawthorn tree which had obviously knocked me down. White blossoms were floating down around me and all I could think was that it must by now be the month of the hawthorn.

Then, when the Eingl were almost within a spearthrow, out of nowhere we heard the pealing of a horn. A moment later there was a sound of galloping and a group of riders burst out of the trees upstream. The Eingl stopped in their tracks. The horsemen swept past us and on towards our pursuers, who suddenly found it their turn to race for their lives. One of the riders stopped beside us and I found myself looking up into the grinning face of Echu Mac Luin.

Pascent helped me to my feet. I was stunned and dizzy but otherwise unhurt. I ran my hands through my hair and released a shower of white blossoms. 'The hawthorn always was an unlucky tree,' I said. 'Any harper will tell you.'

'Are we near the road?' Pascent asked Echu.

'It's just through the trees; we were on it when we heard your horn. We thought you were attacking us.'

Pascent looked at me and shook his head. 'You're a clown Gwion ap Talhearn. What are you?'

'I'm a clown.'

9

Dun Guayrdi

The Eingl might be a people of the hills, but they knew how to make a place impregnable. The evening after our return to the war host I stood with Pascent looking up at Dun Guayrdi. It was set high on a crag of black rock whose north and western faces fell sheer to the fields and pastures below. On its eastern flank grassy dunes rolled down to the sea, and only at its southern tip, where a neck of land led up to the gateway, was it easy to approach. Tall wooden stockades ran around the edge of the dun, except for a short length along the highest edges of the cliff where a thick thorn hedge served just as well. Trails of hearth smoke curled upwards from within the dun as though the encircling war hosts of Rheged and Strathclud were nothing to worry about and life continued as normal.

To the south of the dun the coast ran straight, the forest ending among the dunes which edged the beach, and it was there that Riderch had made camp. To the north the coastline was eaten out by a wide bay, shallow with the silt poured into it by two streams. A low rim of smaller outcrops lay along its southern shore, and it was at the western end of these, above one of the streams, that Urien had made camp amidst the overgrown earthwork of some ancient and long-abandoned settlement. It was separated from Dun Guayrdi by two miles of forest, above which Pascent and I had walked as we followed the rim out to the coast to a knoll about a mile away from the dun.

We found Urien and Owain, Elphin and Llywarch, sitting by three rowan trees which crowned the outcrop and laughing.

'Share the joke,' said Pascent as we joined them.

Urien grinned, the corners of his eyes creased with amusement. 'We were imagining how it would be if we were to try to take this place by siege, and Llywarch suggested that it would take long enough for Owain to have a grandson to accept the surrender. At least we know why they did not try to strike at us on the march. The edge we have in battle comes either from our horses or from surprise, so why should they not wait for us in a place where we could use neither.'

'How are we to take them, then?' asked Pascent. 'Is there no way we could lure them out?'

'We do know they are waiting for us to make the first move.
Rioc came upon a trader who was pushing his horses fast down
the coast in an attempt to get out of the way of things. He said
that he had seen the preparations in Dun Guayrdi. The king of
the Eingl is called Adda, a cunning old fox by all accounts, and
he sits up there now with his sons, one of whom goes by the
name of Aethelric and is perhaps the same man we chased out
of Rheged last summer. They have sent their women and
children to the Isle of Metcaud over the water behind us, and
now they are biding their time and counting their strengths.
I think it is what I would be doing if I were Adda of Bernicia.'

'So?' said Pascent.

Urien's eyes narrowed with something far from laughter. 'So
we do the only thing we can; we come at it from the south and
east and burn our way in.' He pulled a leaf from a rowan twig he
was playing with. 'One way or the other there will be many new
widows by sunset tomorrow.'

I was not the only one who slept badly that night; we were all
grateful when two hours before dawn it came time to be leaving
the camp and taking the track through the forest. Our march was
silent except for the bursts of nervous laughter whenever someone tripped over a root or walked into a tree. The tide was out
when we reached the beach and we fanned out over the flat
sands, gazing upwards at the black shape of the dun set against
the paling sky and the silhouettes of watchers on the stockades.

By the time the far rim of the sea began to turn amber with the
approach of sunrise we had taken up positions in a crescent
around the southern end and eastern flank of the dun, just out of
arrow-range. We kindled an arc of driftwood fires in which our
archers could light the arrows tied with pitch-soaked rags which
they would soon send flying into the timbers of the stockade. The
men of Strathclud waited at the southern end, facing the gateway, while the men of Dalriada and Rheged were strung along
the dunes of the eastern side with our backs to the sea. I was with
Owain, Geraint and Pascent; to our left was Echu and his war
band, some of whom had painted themselves for the occasion
with ochre and scarlet; to our right was Llywarch with the men of
southern Rheged and beyond him Urien and Elphin.

We waited for the daylight to grow in strength and light to give
shape to the hummocks of dune which rose up to the dun, while

the Eingl crowded the ramparts blowing off their deep war horns and shouting what must surely be insulting if we could only understand the language. It had been settled that I would stay with the archers, but I was still sick with fear.

At long last the tip of the rising sun blazed on the horizon behind us. Owain turned to me.

'Gwion, there's just time to ask you for a hunting song.'

I had not expected to be called on to sing and my voice felt as weak as my knees, but memory suddenly brought me one of the songs my father had sung the night of the muster at Caer Brighid. I realised that he and all the men who rode that night were about to be avenged and my voice climbed like a hawk into the sky.

> 'When your father rode out hunting
> Spear on his shoulder
> Club in his hand,
> He'd call his white hounds
> "Giff! Gaff!
> Catch catch! Fetch! fetch!"
> Whatever came near your father's spear
> Unless it had wings
> It could never get clear. . . .'

There was no time for the second verse. Urien had given the signal for the blowing of the war horn, and its call was taken up and repeated all along the line of men. The archers dipped their arrows in the fires and ran forward to loose them. A flight of fire-birds soared over the dunes and thudded into the stockade and the archers ran back to seize another arrow from the clusters which had been stuck point down in the sand. Arrows fired from the ramparts fell short among the dunes; the wind was on our side. It blew the arrows embedded in the stockade into long scarves of flame which licked at the vertical timbers, and the Eingl ran to and fro sluicing down buckets of water to stop fire taking hold. All but two of the fire-arrows had been extinguished when the second flight hit home, and it too was soaked before it could do much damage. The Eingl renewed their jeers and cat-calls.

Owain told some of the archers near us to fire ordinary arrows at the men on the ramparts, but the wind from the sea evidently rose upwards as it struck the dun for the arrows were lifted well over the heads of their targets. Owain cursed and kicked the sand

'Back to fire-arrows,' he shouted, 'only this time send them over the rampart into the dun. Let's see if we can set fire to their halls and bothies and make them use up their water or choke.'

Twelve arrows flew over the stockade and a minute later two plumes of blue smoke began to belch upwards into the sky. The other men of Rheged to our right began to copy us and the smoke quickly grew thicker and the men on the ramparts thinner. To our left the painted warriors of Dalriada stood around looking confused; their skills of warfare were of the screaming charge and spear-play and they could do nothing but wait for the coming of their moment. Their unease ran like a whisper along our lines and men began looking at each other as if asking what there was that we could try next.

Owain turned to me with his hands on his hips. 'What would the Romans have done if they were here?'

'Myrddin says they used to build wooden towers higher than the defences and push them against the ramparts. . . .'

He rolled his eyes and looked skywards.

'I know,' said Pascent. 'We could build a huge wooden horse and hide inside it, pretending to have run away. I know it's been done before, but they do say the Eingl worship white stallions.'

Owain laughed. 'Then they would run out and set fire to it as an offering to their gods.'

We were interrupted by the arrival of Urien, Llywarch and Elphin.

'It's a waste of time trying to set light to the ramparts,' said Urien. 'Let's leave the archers here to try to burn them out from the inside and see what we can do to the main gateway once we are all together.'

The orders were called out and we set off along the dunes while the archers kept to their work. I fell beside my uncle who was wearing his grimmest of expressions.

'How did the Sea Wolves ever take this place?' I asked him.

He smiled sadly. 'It was different then, nothing more than eight bothies and a thorn hedge.'

We were soon massed in one wedge of warriors facing the southern tip of the dun. Above us the gateway ramparts were crowded with archers waiting for us to go within range. Behind them, though, the dun no longer looked impregnable; fire-arrows were still showering down and the thick blue smoke of burning thatch was now a seething cloud billowing over the ramparts of the western side. I squeezed my way through the war host to where the kings were holding council at the edge of the trees.

'There are only two ways of doing this,' Riderch was saying. 'We either wait and hope to exhaust their water so we can burn them out or burn our way in, or we use all we have to thrust through the gateway, which would mean paying a heavy price.'

'I have no wish to throw myself into a rain of their arrows,' said Urien, 'but if we wait there seems the risk that we will run out of arrows before they run out of water.'

'There is a third way,' said Echu Mac Luin.

'What might it be, this third way?' asked Urien.

'You remember how there is a place on the western side where there is no stockade, only thorn hedge?'

'Aye, but it has nothing but cliff below it,' said Riderch.

'I can climb that cliff,' said Echu. 'I have warriors who can climb that cliff. It would be death to do it when the Eingl could see it and shoot us off or knock us off as they chose, but look now, that whole side of the dun is one cloud of smoke. We can climb to the top, cut our way through the hedge, and have our swords deep inside them before they even see us clearly enough to know we are no kinsmen of theirs.'

'If the wind does not change,' said Urien.

'If the wind does not change, and if you keep the fires burning,' replied Echu. 'Let the hosts of Strathclud and Rheged batter at the gateway, and when you hear a horn blow three times, break your way through and we will finish the fight together.'

'How long do you need?' asked Riderch.

'We will make our way round through the trees, and trust you have the Eingl caring only for their gateway when we cross the fields to the foot of the rock. We will be inside the dun in an hour.'

Urien nodded. 'Then let's move while we have the wind with us. Good hunting, brother Echu.'

Echu shouted to two of his companions. 'Fer Rogain, Conare, bring our warriors together.' The men of Dalriada gathered around him. He spoke to them briefly, then they turned and melted into the trees.

'Owain,' said Urien. 'Cut me a tree trunk, ash or young elm. We will be needing a battering ram. Elphin, Pascent, tell the men to make ready for the charge. Make as much noise as you can.'

Thirty minutes later the war hosts were gathered below the gateway, an ash-trunk like a giant's spear being nursed by the men in the centre of the press. The ramparts above were packed tight with Eingl silhouetted against the ever-growing cloud of smoke. I looked at the slopes of duned sand which led up to the gateway; they would make hard climbing, and the distance of a bowshot between our war host and the dun would make for a charge of at least five minutes, a charge straight into a rain of arrows. Smoke was still belching out over the western side of the ramparts, and from where we stood we watched what the Eingl could not see, a line of men racing through the fields of ripening barley towards the foot of the rock. That was the signal Urien and Riderch had been waiting for, and at the sight of it they blew their horns and unleashed the war hosts, who in one horde began their rush up the dunes.

From the very beginning it was a desperate chaos. It was impossible to keep any sort of order while struggling for a footing in the sand, and as the arrows shrieked down from the ramparts they had only to strike one man for him to tumble backwards and knock those behind him off their feet. By the time the host was cresting the second of the seven dunes which rose like waves to the gateway it had already left a trail of more than thirty dead or wounded men. Our own archers were running forward now to loose arrows amongst the defenders, distracting their aim if nothing more, but our charge still seemed to lose a man for every yard gained. The damage was worst at the centre, where the task of heaving the battering ram over the dunes slowed men down and made them easy targets. I could only stand by the trees, watching their painfully slow progress and begging success from every god I knew by name.

They crested the third dune and spilled into the hollow below the fourth; half-way there. I was conscious both of the one moving mass of warriors and of the individuals I knew caught up in its nightmare endeavour. I could see Urien, Elphin and Myrddin by the Red Dragon banner near the front, Owain and Geraint among those hauling the battering ram upwards, and in the scrambling swirl around them I could recognise my uncle by his old smithy-sweat-darkened leather tunic and Pascent by his tuft of red hair and the mail shirt he had won as booty at Catraeth. My eyes darted from one to the other, checking that they were still moving, terrified as I was that I might lose sight of one of them and see him again among the sprawled bodies the charge was leaving in its wake. Now I understood my mother's lack of spirit for what we were doing. I no longer wanted Dun Guayrdi to fall so Bryneich could be freed of the Eingl, I wanted it to fall so that those I loved could come out of the battle alive.

At the top of the seventh dune they met the heaviest barrage yet, with spears and throwing-axes joining the flights of arrows. Over a dozen men fell in the space of a single breath, but the rest pushed on across the levelled ground before the gateway. They began to form a dark mass against the rampart of the dun, like bees swarming on a honeycomb, their shields raised above their heads for protection against the waterfall of death the Eingl poured down on them. I heard the thud of the battering ram against the gate, then another, then the sound was lost amidst the tumult of yells and screams. Our archers were now high on the dunes themselves, and striking at the defenders with growing accuracy, but men were going down fast by the gateway while the gate itself refused to be breached. If the butchery from above continued much longer our host could be reduced to a mess of blood and rags which the Eingl would be able to finish off with a charge of their own. I clenched my fists until my nails dug into my palms.

In desperation I tore my eyes away from the carnage going on above me and looked out to sea. A mile from the shore a long tall-prowed rowing-boat was pulling towards the beach. It must be coming from the Isle of Metcaud, which lay in the distance behind it. In the same moment that I saw it I heard, high inside the dun, three clear notes on a hunting horn. Echu had succeeded. A great cheer went up from the host by the gateway, and it had no time to ebb before I heard a splintering crash and saw the gates of Dun Guayrdi shudder, then swing open. We were through.

The war host surged through the gateway. The Eingl vanished from the ramparts, and suddenly all I could see was the shape of the dun beneath the smoke and the trail of fallen men down the dunes beneath it. It came to me that the boat might be bringing fresh warriors who if they landed and moved up to the now empty gateway could take our host from behind. The boat was still some way offshore, which left me time to give warning, so I left the trees and began running up the dunes.

I took a path to the left of that followed by the charge as I knew I could bear neither to see the dead nor ignore the pleas of the wounded. As I climbed I breathed in gasps and my legs felt weak; it was almost mid-morning and I had eaten nothing since the evening before. That proved just as well, as when I crested the seventh dune and wheezed upright in front of the gateway I saw things to make me spew. Bodies lay tangled and lifeless, stuck with arrows or broken by throwing-axes. Inside the gateway there was nothing but smoke and the sounds of battle, and the stench of burning stung my throat and eyes. I began to make my way through the fallen, over faces I had seen smiling as I sang by the fires of our camps, and I had almost reached the gateway when I saw Geraint ap Riwal, quite dead, staring into the sky.

I think I was kneeling beside him when I heard a thunder of hoofbeats coming towards me from inside the dun. A group of horsemen took shape in the smoke and galloped out of it towards the gateway. At their head rode the tawny-maned man I had seen a year before by the river Lleven; Aethelric, prince of Bernicia. For an instant I stared transfixed, then realised I was in the centre of their path and scrambled wildly over the fallen bodies to where the dune fell away. They were out of the gateway, ten of them, before I had time to drop into the grass, but they had not thoughts to waste on killing the likes of me and sent their horses plunging down the dunes in the direction of the beach.

Some of the archers were still posted below the dun, and they loosed a flight of arrows which took two of the riders. The rest, with Aethelric still leading them, reached the flat sands and headed for the sea where the rowing-boat was reaching the shallows. I watched them splash through the waves and clamber on board, leaving their horses up to their flanks in the sea. Only as the boat began to pull away from the shore did it dawn on me that if Aethelric the prince had fled then Adda the king must have fallen and Dun Guayrdi be ours.

I went through the gateway and made my way past burning bothies and a litter of corpses to the northern end of the dun, which had no bothies and was free of smoke. It was there that the Eingl had made their last stand and it was there now that the men of Rheged, Strathclud and Dalriada were ending the battle. The fight had been vicious. I found the well and drew water; some of the men were so weary they stretched out on the turf beside the dead. The day was turning hot and the air beginning to swarm with flies. Owain walked past me towards the gateway, his hands scrubbed raw by the battering ram. He did not see me, and I knew he was going to find Geraint.

The battle was over before midday, but it was late afternoon before we had sorted out the wreckage it left. The Eingl wounded had been cured with quick knives, but ours had to wait while we had horses brought down to ferry them back to the camp; we had no plans to spend the night among the burnt out remains of Dun Guayrdi. My uncle had received an axe-gash in his right thigh. It had taken tight binding to end the bleeding and it would need all Fionn's powers if he were ever to walk easily again. He would never again take part in a war trail, but I do not think he was sad about that; he had fought the last fight that mattered.

We piled the Eingl dead into the hollows between the dunes, the grizzled body of Adda among them, and left them to the hungrily gathering ravens. Our own dead we buried in two long graves on the landward side of the rock. There were many of them. Over one hundred and fifty of the men of Rheged had fallen, leaving Urien with only three hundred warriors, and some of them would not be fighting any more battles that summer. At least Urien had his sons, for Riderch was burying Rioc along with some hundred and thirty warriors of Strathclud. The heaviest price of any one kin had been paid by Echu, who in taking the dun his own way had lost half the men who had ridden with him out of Dalriada.

As the graves were filled in Elphin recited the Christian prayers of burial while above us the charred and still-smoking ramparts of the dun began to glow as the sun sank lower in the sky. We stood dumbly around the graves, each man with his own grief, but each man thanking his own gods that we had won and that we lived. When the prayers were finished, Urien spoke.

'I want to leave the brothers we bury here with a vow. We will not join them at the endless feasting in Caer Sidhi until we are worthy to sit and drink beside them, and we will not be worthy until we finish this trail on which they have died. The last of the Eingl of Bryneich have been driven from the coast, and their only foothold now is the Isle of Metcaud. We must go there and burn them out. We must drive them beyond the ninth wave of the sea.'

10

The Old Curse

It was easier said than done. We spent the day after the taking of Dun Guayrdi hunting for food. Our horses were fresh even if their riders were exhausted, and foraging parties rode into the woods to track down boar and deer, and returned with an added catch of fifteen cattle who had been left to wander when the Eingl abandoned their settlements in the face of our advance. Only on the following morning did Owain and Echu ride out to reconnoitre the coast facing the Isle of Metcaud, and the news they brought back was not of the best.

Metcaud was not so much an island as a promontory of the coastline with low land behind it which had been invaded by the sea. This had created a tidal lagoon shaped like an arrowhead, with the island lying along the right-hand edge of the blade, separated from the coast by a wide bay of low-tide mudflats fed by several streams and a river called the Lleu. Only at the tip of the arrowhead was there an obvious line of access to the island; a narrow spar of dunes leading out towards it, broken in two places by tidal channels, the wider of which separated Metcaud from the rest of Britain. Owain judged that it could perhaps be waded at low water, but it would be impossible for horses and it would only take a handful of alert archers on the far shore to turn the crossing into a disaster. There were no boats, of course, the Eingl had seen to that, nor had we any way of knowing how many men Aethelric had with him; whether he had only women and children, or whether he had enough warriors to meet us in force wherever we landed. All we knew was that in the early evening the smoke from a good number of cooking fires curled upwards into the sky.

There was little Urien could do except send raiders along the coast in both directions in search of boats and make a move of camp which tightened our grip on the island. He sent Echu and Owain, with the men of Dalriada and half the men of Rheged, to make camp at the end of the spar dunes. Riderch and the men of Strathclud joined Urien at the camp in the old earthwork, which was only a short ride from the southern tip of the bay of Metcaud. Between the two camps lay some ten miles of coastline, dunes and pine trees leading back to denser woodland, broken only by the swampy mouth of the Lleu. Here and there were the clearings of abandoned Eingl steadings and the overgrown earthworks of forgotten people who had lived on these shores before ever it was Bryneich and ruled by the kings of Caer Brighid. Sometimes I woke in the middle of the night to hear the soughing of the wind in the trees and the grumble of the tides and felt as much of a stranger as I had in my first days in Caer Lugualid. I forgot what had brought us here, and forgot even that I had been born and raised less than a day's ride to the west.

On the fifth day after the battle we had found neither boats nor a safe way over the mudflats to Metcaud. Food was running short again and around the campfires there was once more the sense of restlessness which I remembered from the waiting at Catraeth. Urien gave orders for the wounded to return to Rheged, those who could to ride on horseback and the rest in mule carts, and for Pascent to ride with them to levy both fresh warriors and food. Pascent sulked all night at the thought of leaving the war trail, oblivious to the fact that he had just been given his first command, but the next morning he was at the head of the small column as it creaked inland towards the Roman road which would take it to Caer Lugualid in seven days. My uncle was stretched out in one of the carts and it was good to think that he would soon be back with Fionn and little Dichuil.

I was almost useless as a harper by this time. Since leaving Rheged I had sung and told all the songs I knew many times over, and had little to offer the warriors when they gathered by the evening fires unless they called for an old favourite. Only Myrddin and Llywarch had a depth of knowledge in which to find new songs and tales, or craft enough to weave the old tales into something which seemed new, so I put my harp away and sat by one or the other of them to learn what I could. So it was that I was with Myrddin by the fire of the kings when Morcant came.

He came with a hundred horsemen on an evening so calm that we heard his horses in the forest when they were still some way away. He dismounted outside the earthwork and strode in towards our fire, accompanied by Caw his harper and a man who looked ugly enough to be his brother, and when he saw Urien and Riderch he grinned and held out his arms in greeting. Neither of them rose, so he squatted down to face them across the fire.

'So my brothers, I am come,' he beamed.

'You have been long in coming,' returned Riderch.

'You sent me no word,' he complained, holding out his hands.

Riderch smiled. 'You tell me that you need word of what takes place within a day's ride of your own hunting runs, or do you tell me that you heard no whisper when I rode out of Strathclud half a moon ago?'

He laughed, showing his teeth. 'I tell you neither. I had word that the Picts were thinking of their own war trail and judged it best to ride to my northern borders to discourage them from coming south into either Manau Goddodin or Strathclud.'

Riderch smiled again. 'I find it strange that I have not heard the same when I left Rathmail my foster-brother in Strathclud to send me just such news as this.'

'He must have wished not to distract you.' Morcant slapped his thighs. 'Enough of this teasing. Imagine my horror when I heard that Dun Guayrdi had fallen before I had time to ride south and join in the battle. "Morcant," I said to myself, "if you do not make haste to these lands you have dreamed so long of freeing, your brothers will have made the kill without you." So I rode at one, bringing only the handful of men who were with me at the time, and here I am at last.'

'It is sad you delayed so long,' said Urien quietly. 'Those who do not know you might be forgiven for supposing you had waited to hear what took place at Dun Guayrdi before deciding whether or not it was a war trail worth your while to follow.'

Morcant almost winced at this, and an edgy silence fell around the fire. After a moment he levelled his turnip-coloured eyes on Urien. 'Just as those who do not know you, Urien ap Cynvarch, might be forgiven for thinking that you have become drunk on victory and wish to keep Bryneich for yourself instead of returning it to the one who is its rightful king by blood.'

'You have no claim to Bryneich either by blood or deed,' said Urien. 'You had no friendship for Outigern when he was king and you did not lift a spear to help him when the Eingl took this kingdom for themselves. Do you really think we spat blood at Dun Guayrdi just to give it to you when the time seemed right to you to come and collect it?'

Morcant raised his eyes to the skies and made a gesture of lament. 'Urien, my brother-in-arms in this long struggle against the Eingl, it is wrong that we use words like knives. I have ridden hard, you have fought hard and bravely, and we are both tired. As I rode here I asked myself in all simplicity; "Morcant, who is to rule Bryneich once it is free? It cannot be my brother Urien, whose own lands are so far away to the south-west. It cannot be my brother Riderch, who I learn to my deep sorrow has lost his son on the war trail. No Morcant," I said to myself, "you are the one whose kingdom and Bryneich lie together like lovers in a bed, you are the one who must accept this task." Such is my thinking.'

He sat back and leered out his smile, while both Urien and Riderch sat looking coldly at him. I remembered how Morcant had leered at Branwen, and I believe that at that moment I felt more hatred for Morcant Dhu of Manau Goddodin than I could ever feel for Aethelric and all the Sea Wolves who had ever sailed. I could sense that hostility was now running like a cold current through all who sat by the fire. When Urien finally spoke he spoke for all of us, but even I was surprised by the aching disgust in his voice.

'We shame our own dead by sitting with the likes of you. Take your men and leave, now, and if you ever again come south of the Tuid into Bryneich, expect to be treated how you used to be treated, as a cattle-thief.'

Morcant's face sagged with disbelief. He looked over the fire and was met by Urien's grey stare. Awkwardly, as though drunk, he lurched to his feet followed by his companions.

'I will kill you for that,' he muttered.

'You would have to,' said Urien, 'for I will die before I take back those words.'

Morcant's threat was hollow, and his awareness of the fact seethed on his face. We outnumbered his men by four to one. He did the only thing he could do; he turned on his heel and strode off towards his horsemen, who were still waiting outside the earthwork. We heard them gallop away into the forest.

'It is a bad thing that has happened here tonight,' said Riderch. 'We built our war trail on a brotherhood of all the Celtic kingdoms, and now that is broken. It is the old curse.'

Urien nodded. 'Yet there was nothing else to say to him.'

'No,' agreed Riderch. 'You spoke for us all.'

'Myrddin,' said Urien, 'sing something to wash away the sourness.'

Myrddin looked down at the harp lying across his lap. It was the only time I ever saw him lost for a song.

The next morning I rode out with Urien, Myrddin and some of

the king's companions to the spit of dunes which formed the southern tip of the bay of Metcaud. The tide was beginning to ebb and brown dunlin gulls were hopping along the water's edge in search of food. Metcaud itself was here only a mile away across the water. We could see men moving among the bothies of the settlement, and the wind carried to us the odd shout and the smell of cooking fires. Urien was intent on the boats drawn up on the beach below the settlement.

He turned to Llywarch. 'Do you think we have enough good swimmers to cross in darkness when the tide is high and to steal those boats?'

'A hard one, that,' replied Llywarch. 'If they have too many people sleeping there for them to house some may sleep in the boats, and either way I should think they keep a sharp night-watch.'

'Still, we must get those boats somehow or we'll still be here at Samhain,' groaned Urien.

He was interrupted by the arrival of a rider at the landward end of the dune-spit, driving his horse fast towards us along the firm sand at the water's edge. Urien and Llywarch climbed to the top of a dune to look down on him as he approached and reined to a halt.

'My lord Urien, I bring a message from Owain,' he shouted. 'The lord of the Eingl named Aethelric crossed to the shore this morning. He wishes to speak with you and ask your mercy for himself and his people.'

'Does he indeed?' said Urien. 'Where is he now?'

'At the north camp with Owain, who bids you come as quickly as you can.'

We ran back to where our horses were grazing half-heartedly on the tough grass of the dunes, and in a few moments were galloping along the southern shores of the bay. Urien rode beside the messenger.

'Have you been to the south camp?' he asked.

'No, my lord. Owain told me to ride by the coast in the hope of finding you sooner.'

Urien turned in the saddle. 'Llywarch, will you ride to the south camp and tell Riderch to follow us with all speed.'

Llywarch grinned. 'With such news as this I would ride to Caer Legion and beyond.' A few minutes later we reached the inner shore of the bay and Llywarch turned inland while we took the northern track. The summer foliage of the trees made a patchwork roof over our heads and we rode through a tunnel of dappled sunlight. Whenever the trees broke to our right we could see the Isle of Metcaud across the ebbing waters of the bay, a challenge we would no longer have to meet. Myrddin, who rode beside me, began to sing in the saddle.

Soon we had covered half the distance to Owain's camp and were coming out of the trees onto the marshy banks of the river Lleu. We slowed our horses to canter across the reed-beds which led to the soft ford, and had almost reached it when the messenger turned his horse across the track and motioned for us to halt. He turned to face us and I saw that he was laughing.

'What is this?' asked Urien.

'The end,' replied the messenger.

Suddenly there were men with spears running out of the far trees. A flight of arrows came over their heads and landed amongst us. Urien coughed and fell backwards out of the saddle with an arrow in his throat and an arrow in his chest. Two of his companions fell with him. Elphin turned his horse, yelling at us to get back, but then a spear caught him between the shoulders and he collapsed over his horse's neck. Myrddin and I backed wildly, the hooves of our horses sinking into the marshy ground. I heard Myrddin cry out and turned to see him reeling as he clutched at a spear that had taken him in the stomach. His horse reared up and crashed down on Faencha with such force that I was thrown sideways out of the saddle. My shoulder slammed into a rotten log among the reeds, Faencha shrieked and fell on top of me, and everything went black.

11

Waning Moon

The first thing I knew was a heart-beat, only it was beating on the inside of my head as though my brain were a bull's hide drum. Then I felt a pain in my ribs, which hurt me at every breath and whose keenness measured the life left in my body. I lay still, waiting for the beating in my head to end, but it did not wish to. I felt cold night air on my face and listened to the sounds around me; someone breathing in gasps to my right, and some way away the crackling of fires and voices raised in anger. I peeled back my eyelids and blinked wide in the cold as I stared up into a sky of bright stars. Turning my head I saw someone squatting beside a figure stretched out on the ground. The kneeling figure turned towards me and rose hurriedly to come to my side. It was Llywarch.

'Gwion,' he said, 'you are back with us?'

I tried to collect and arrange my memories from before the darkness. I knew I was in the camp of the earthwork, but I knew vaguely that it was not where I had been when the darkness struck.

'What happened?' I asked.

'It was a trap. The rider was not from Owain but from the men of Manau Goddodin. It was they who ambushed you.'

'The others?'

'Myrddin lies over there in deep wound-fever. The others, Urien, Elphin, are all dead. You are lucky. Your ribs are bruised, perhaps cracked, but there is no other wound that we can see. It seems that Faencha took the spear which was meant for you.'

The nightmare came back to me. 'I should be dead,' I moaned.

'Don't be a fool. There has been enough death today.' He reached out for a wooden bowl. 'Drink this.' He crooked an arm under my back and raised me until I could take the bowl and sip through my dry lips. It was water with a tang of bitter herbs, so cold that it made me shiver. Llywarch lowered me to the ground again and pulled my cloak up under my chin. 'Now sleep,' he said.

I lay looking up at the stars. I tried to summon my memories but all I could think of was the pain in my ribs and the numbness

85

of the rest of my body. After a moment my eyes closed and the darkness returned.

When I awoke the dawn was still fresh and I was soaked with dew. My head, at least, felt clear. There was commotion all around me, and as I sat up I saw that the cooking fires had been allowed to fall into ashes and not relit for the morning meal. Horses were being saddled at the gateway of the earthwork. I tried to spring to my feet and found myself swaying dizzily on my heels.

I stumbled towards the main knot of men, but before I reached them Owain broke away and came towards me. He looked like a stranger; his eyes were wide and red-rimmed and his face pale and drawn as though he had not slept. He placed a hand on each of my shoulders, as if we both needed holding steady, and began to speak rapidly.

'Gwion, the war host is riding for Manau Goddodin.'

'My horse is dead. . . .'

'You're not coming with us. I am leaving you Myrddin's horse and I am leaving you Myrddin. Llywarch tells me he has only a few days to live, that it might be kindness if we ended it for him now, but neither you nor I could do that. I cannot take you with me on the trail I start today, so I am leaving you the last mule cart. You know Bryneich; take him somewhere safe and see him through to death, then make your own way back to Caer Lugualid.'

'Will you not come back here?'

'One day, yes, to finish what my father began, but it will not be this summer. I am riding now to find Morcant Dhu and to flay him alive, and if I have to I'll chase him to the northern edge of Britain. You have the gold arm-rings I gave you at the rath on the Wall?'

'Yes.'

'Keep them. There is also a warrior to help you, one of your own people who was a thrall on Metcaud but who swam over to join us at the north camp. I leave him to help you.' He paused. 'That is all then. The sun and the moon be on your path, Gwion.'

'And on yours,' I murmured.

I walked beside him to the throng of horsemen massed by the gateway. He called out to a spindly figure in tattered breeks who was leaning on a spear, and who loped towards us with a red weal round his neck where a thrall-ring had evidently been cut away. I wondered who had done the job in my uncle's absence, then thought I saw something flicker in the stranger's eyes and recognised Uaran. We stared at each other speechlessly.

As soon as Owain was in the saddle the war host began to move out onto the forest trail, and within minutes it disappeared into the trees, the sound of hooves being slowly replaced by the wind in the pines and the morning birdsong. I looked around the earthwork, at the mule cart, Myrddin's horse, Uaran, the figure of Myrddin stretched out under a cloak, the grey holes made in the turf by the faintly smoking cooking fires, and the litter of ten days' occupation. Urien had chosen it as the camp from which to free Bryneich, and now it and Bryneich were being abandoned as Owain rode away on his inescapable blood feud. It was the place where I had come closest to my dreams and the place where all my dreams had died. I hope no-one ever sets foot there again.

Uaran and I should have had much to tell each other, but that first day we spoke little. Myrddin was deep in fever, lost to the daylight, so we lifted him into the mule cart as carefully as we could and set off inland. At first I tried to ride his horse, but even though Ossian was a calm old stallion he was too hard on my ribs, so I climbed onto the mule cart beside Uaran where I only had to endure the odd sickening lurch. We followed the Roman road north till it was crossed by the old tribal track from the coast to Dod Law, and up that we turned, climbing slowly away from the sea. At one moment when I looked round to check on Myrddin, I saw Metcaud lying on its cloak of blue, and I wondered if Aethelric knew yet that the threat was over and his kingdom of Bernicia safe for another winter, perhaps for ever.

The ride grew harder as our climb grew steeper. We had no trouble with the mule, who kept to a steady pull up the centre of the track, but he could not keep the wheels from bouncing over the tree-roots and rain-ruts which veined the earth. I had forgotten my ribs now, and pushed the dark shock of the day before to the bottom of my mind; what ruled my thoughts was the problem of getting Myrddin safely to Caer Brighid so the women might do all they could to heal him. All I knew was that I could not let him die. He was still deep in fever-sleep, silent but for the occasional sigh or groan, but he was beginning to glisten with sweat.

It was late afternoon before we pulled out of larch woods onto the open moor of Dod Law, and saw beneath us the valley of the Till and on the far side Caer Brighid set against the clumped hills which rolled down from the high back of Yr Cerrid. Uaran stopped the cart near some of the boulders marked with the ancient spirals of death-in-life and life-in-death and leapt down onto the young heather. He was breathing the hill air in gulps, rubbing his hands round the red ring on his neck and grinning from ear to ear.

'By all the gods, Gwion! It is five summers since I last saw Caer Brighid.'

I nodded. 'It has changed now,' I said, 'and I'm afraid we must camp here for the night if we want Myrddin to reach it alive tomorrow.'

He laughed, then climbed back onto the cart to take us to the deserted settlement a few spearthrows distant. 'I do not care how much it has changed, nor if it takes us a moon to reach it. I never thought I would be free to journey anywhere again. I could kiss the feet of your lords of Rheged.'

'I'm glad,' I said numbly.

So we made our own hearth on Dod Law that night, and I poured a trickle of water down Myrddin's throat. Uaran stood looking west, leaning on the spear which he told me Owain had given him. He was still there when I fell asleep.

The middle of the next afternoon saw our mule cart creaking up the hill track towards Caer Brighid. The final slope below the gateway had always made a challenge for the finest riders of the tribe; for the cart it was out of the question, so we left Myrddin on the shoulder and led Ossian and the mule up to where the women were standing in the gateway of the rath. A moment later we were running back down the slope to carry Myrddin up slung between us in the fallen hanging from the king's hall, and it was in the king's hall that we laid him.

I told our story to my mother and Eorann as they unwound the clotted bandages from Myrddin's stomach and did what they could to clean the mess the spear had made. He lay senseless, his gaunt chest heaving with every breath.

'I have some salves,' I said hopefully.

'This is not a wound to be healed by salves,' said Eorann.

I kindled a fire where once the kill of Outigern's hunts had been roasted for the king's feasting, and sat by Myrddin willing him to live. My mother brought me food when the women had cooked and sat with me while I ate. We talked awkwardly. It was as though we had lost each other the day five summers before that I left Caer Brighid with my uncle, and neither of us now had the strength to pull back the curtain which had been drawn between us. She asked more questions about the happenings on the coast, but asked nothing of what I would do now; the future was suspended until we knew whether or not Myrddin would be a part of it.

The wound-fever ruled him through the night. The next day was the hottest the year had yet given. There was little I could do except wipe the sweat from his face and neck with a wet rag. It hurt me to look at his face, his eyes seemed sunken and his cheeks hollow. I watched and waited. I thought of his singing against the wind in the sacred grove by Caer Lugualid, I heard again his voice lift and his words fly as he urged Urien to ride for Brigantia, and it was as though I were counting over how much he had become to me in the four winters that he had been my teacher, and, through the harp, my second father.

Towards evening his breathing became harsher, more strained, as though his body had more to fight. Finally it was too much to listen to and I went and stood in the doorway of the hall and looked north over the valley of the Tuid to the far hills of Manau Goddodin. In the distance were two black trails of smoke like a pair of crow's tail feathers someone had stuck into the rim of the horizon, and I knew that Owain was taking his vengeance.

Suddenly the harsh breathing behind me stopped, and I spun round to see that Myrddin's eyes were open and staring up at me. I ran to him, lifted his head and gave him as much water as I dared. As I settled him again he smiled wanly and his lips cracked.

'Myrddin, Myrddin, you've come back.'

'Till the moonrise.'

'But the fever has left you.'

He gulped and swallowed, and moistening his mouth. 'The fever has won. All I have is a pool of stillness before the end.'

I shook my head. 'No, you must fight it and you must live. I could not bear it if you died.'

His face was too weak to show expression, but he placed a long-fingered hand lightly over mine, which were clenched on my knees. 'It is my time, Gwion. Accept that as I have.' He closed his eyes. 'If I had died five summers ago, after the battle of Arderydd, I would have died leaving no-one to sing my songs. Now I have had you these last four winters I can go knowing I leave a harper behind me. That is good.'

'But if you die I will never be a harper,' I wailed. 'You know it takes as many years as there are months in a year to learn the songs. I have hardly begun.'

'You have begun, and that is what matters,' he said quietly. 'Others can teach you the rest. There is Llywarch if he is still alive when autumn comes. If he falls, go to Gwynedd. They have always had good harpers there, and they will welcome you as kin.'

'I don't want another kingdom. Bryneich is lost, Urien is dead . . . you are all the kin I want.'

His hand tightened on mine until his grip was like a claw. 'You have my songs. Listen to me, and remember what I say. Urien was not one to lurk in Rheged until the Eingl hunted him down like an old boar in a thicket. Be proud of all he has done, and that he died on a war trail of his own choosing. Kings are of the Sun, they die as surely as the Sun dies at the end of each year and their glory grows out of leaving a good harvest behind them. . . . We are not kings, we are harpers, and the harp-kind have only the kingdom of the Moon. It is the Moon who gives us songs and the Moon who is our lover, and in belonging to her we have an older allegiance than we owe to any Sun-lord who grants us shelter and bids us sing. . . . I have seen many things fall in my time, you have seen two and you will see others. With the passing of each something is lost, but you will always have the songs if you are true to the Moon.'

His grip relaxed and fresh sweating broke out over his face. When he spoke again his voice was fainter. 'I give you a Moon-name, I call you Taliesin. Bury with me the Gwion who is now so empty, and may Taliesin sing strong and true for many years, and never forget how he came by his name. . . .'

A convulsion seized him and he gasped, clutching his stomach with his hands. When it left him he seemed to sink into the ground. 'Oh my Lady,' he whispered, 'sweet cruel Arianrhod. . . .' He breathed out a long sigh which grew fainter into soundlessness, then his head rolled onto its side.

I felt for his heartbeat but could find none. He lay perfectly still. I groaned and turned away to stagger to the doorway of the hall. On the northern horizon there was now a third plume of black smoke, and I saw that the moon was rising above the ridge of Yr Cerrid; a pale waning left-hand moon. Near at hand I heard a girl's laugh, and turned to see Emer and Uaran sitting hand in hand by a fallen-in bothy. They raised their hands to wave to me, but by that time I was curled up on the ground. Huge sobs were kicking in my stomach and raking through me till I shuddered. I heard Emer and Uaran running towards me, felt their hands on my shoulders, but I was beyond them, beating the earth with my fists as I wept.

When the sun set I was squatting by the fire in my mother's bothy, with Uaran beside me and the women sitting on the far side of the hearth. The women had raised no keening for Myrddin, he was after all only a stranger to them, but his death left a silence in which everyone ate keeping their thoughts to themselves. I scooped away at a bowl of stew with a hunk of barley bannock, knowing that however much I ate I would still feel empty. From time to time I glanced at the others. Old Eorann was engrossed in her meal and Emer and Uaran only had eyes for each other. My mother was also watching Emer and Uaran, but at moments our eyes met and I found myself looking away. I knew I would be leaving, and I knew also that if we looked too deeply into each other's eyes this second parting would be cruel for both of us. Harper or not I could think of no words with which to tell her, and I must have glowed with gratitude when at the end of the meal she brought the subject up herself.

'It cannot be long before the Sea Wolves are riding freely again, and when they are they may well come here. You had best be leaving in the morning.'

'What will they do?' I asked.

'Nothing. There are no traces of any war host to lick them into anger. We will not be here when they come, and we will be here again when they have gone.'

'Where will you go?' Uaran asked me.

'Back the Rheged, to Caer Lugualid.'

'Is it a road the mule cart could take?'

I knew by his face and by the arch of Emer's eyebrows the question which would follow my answer, so I answered both. 'If you can get the mule cart over Yr Cerrid by the ridgeway track, you will find Roman roads to lead you the rest of the way to Rheged. I would be glad of companions, and Caer Lugualid has its own empty bothies where you and Emer could make your hearth.'

He and Emer vanished into each other's eyes again. I looked into the fire a moment then touched him on the wrist. 'Before we make plans for that, will you help me dig a grave?'

'Of course,' he replied. 'Where shall we make it?'

I had not thought of that. Once more it was my mother who saved me.

'Bury him where he lies, in the floor of the feast-hall,' she said. 'It is a good place for a harper to be, a place where songs were sung, and when the timbers have rotted and fallen in and Caer Brighid is no more than a bare hilltop, then he will have the wind to listen to.' She took a torch from the wall of the bothy, lit it in the fire and handed it to Uaran. 'I will come with you.'

Uaran walked ahead to light the torches in the hall and my mother walked beside me with a plaid shawl drawn tightly around her shoulders.

'Why do you not come with us?' I asked.

She looked up at the high hills. 'Perhaps because Eorann is too old to come and too old to be left alone, and I am neither.'

'You will not hate me for leaving you again?'

'It will not be quite so hard this time, and besides, I have seen enough women live on without their sons to know how to do it,' she said proudly. We walked on, but the air was heavy with something unspoken. She sighed. 'To know you are alive and living how your father would have wanted you to live, that cuts the edge off my loneliness. Do not ask me any more questions. You go with every blessing I can give you.'

I tried to find some reply, but we had already reached the doorway of the hall. 'Bury your friend,' she said. 'I will go and prepare food for the journey.'

Uaran and I dug a grave where my father used to set his harper's stool, and there we laid Myrddin. I looked down on his face and said a last farewell, and then placed on his chest the harp he had made for me. His own, with all its magic, I would keep for myself.

12

The Song

I had never taken full measure of my dream of Bryneich. Only as I left it forever, as I crossed the summit of Yr Cerrid and lost sight of Caer Brighid and the sea beyond, did I learn the depths to which the roots of it ran in me. I had too much time to think as our tiny caravan went on its way, the mule cart creaking up the same slopes down which Pascent and I had galloped like the Wild Hunt. Even old Ossian seemed to ache with every step, perhaps because he sensed that every hill we crossed took him further from his old master, perhaps because he sensed that his new rider had a darkening spirit and a breaking heart.

It seemed too, as we reached the Roman road and turned south, that I was growing weaker as though the dream had been my power and that it was slowly ebbing away with each mile I put between myself and Bryneich. When we made camp, in the same places Cialgrin had chosen five summers before, I curled up in my cloak, leaving Uaran and Emer to make a fire and cook for themselves. When I ate I could hardly taste the food, and when we passed through the Wall at the rath where the warriors of Rheged and Strathclud had hosted, I sensed ghosts among the heather and felt myself one of them. I think it was the next day, early in the afternoon, as the sun beat down from a sky of blue as rich as the enamel inlay of a brooch, that the world began to spin around me and I fell off my horse.

I lost myself in a spiralling nightmare. I was with the full war host in the swamp of the river Lleu — The rain came down as it had at Catraeth only it was made up of the arrows that had rained from the ramparts of Dun Guayrdi — Myrddin had been killed and the men of Rheged called me to sing a song but I could not as the breathing sickness was choking my chest and I could not remember how to play the harp — The arrows came down and I was the only one left alive — Branwen appeared screaming 'Why could you not sing for my father?' and began to claw at my face with her fingernails — She ran away from me and only then did my chest clear so that I could talk — I began to run after her but the swamp now stretched in all directions and the mist had come down — I lost all trace of her and ran around in circles — The swamp began to suck at my legs and I felt myself swallowed by the earth.

The night around me was filled with birdsong so rich and beautiful that nine harps in harmony could not have made such music. Light flooded down through my eyelids and I opened my eyes to find myself in a square room which could only be Roman, with Emer's freckled face bending over me and smiling.

'Welcome back,' she said.

'Where have the birds gone?' I asked.

She frowned. 'There are no birds here.' I looked through a stone doorway to see nothing but open moor and guessed I must be in one of the signal towers on the Wall.

'I heard a beautiful birdsong,' I mumbled.

'Perhaps they were the birds of Rhiannon, who make men forget,' she smiled. 'I hope so. You screamed dark things in your sleep.'

I sat up and rubbed my eyes. 'How long have I been asleep?'

'You've been in the fever for seven days.'

I groaned. 'Seven days. Where is Uaran?'

'Hunting. He will soon be back.'

When he returned he showed immense relief at my recovery, and I remembered where we were and that my task was to get Uaran and Emer to Caer Lugualid before Aethelric swept along the road on his own trail of revenge. I crawled into the mule cart and we resumed our journey. My strength trickled back, and I was riding on Ossian when we reached the edge of the hills and looked down on the green forests and plains of Rheged.

I drew rein and heard the mule cart grind to a halt behind me. Turning in the saddle I saw Uaran and Emer gazing at the view with light in their faces; perhaps they saw in it the same reflection of Bryneich which had once struck me. 'Welcome to Rheged,' I said, remembering Geraint. I wanted at once to be back in Caer Lugualid to see how it went with the living, but the best my impatience could allow itself was to nudge Ossian into a canter so that the cart clattered and Emer giggled as Uaran tried desperately to get the mule to keep up with me.

We reached Caer Lugualid early in the evening. The gate guard was a young warrior named Collen who strode towards us as we rattled over the bridge.

'Gwion!' he exclaimed. 'We thought you must be dead.'

'You all returned?' I asked.

'Almost half a moon ago, by the road from Strathclud. Owain

thought you would be here, and Pascent nearly strangled him when he heard you had been left in Bryneich.'

'They are both here now?'

'You should find them in the hall.'

I rode on up the street, while behind me Uaran and Emer wondered at the strange buildings. The square was quiet but for one or two warriors lounging on the side with the most of the weakening sunlight who hailed me as I dismounted. I heard footsteps running from the hall behind me, two hands gripped my shoulders and spun me round and the next thing I knew Pascent was hugging me.

'What took you so long?' he shouted, shaking me till my teeth rattled. 'I had visions of the Wolves chasing you across Pennuin and you riding into another hawthorn tree.'

'I only came back to stop you strangling Owain,' I replied.

'How do you know about that?'

'Harpers know everything.'

'Except where to look when they're riding.' He looked over my shoulder. 'Are these your friends?'

'They are. This is Uaran, who swam over from Metcaud with a thrall-ring round his neck. This is Emer, who you met at Caer Brighid but who has blossomed since then.'

'Indeed. You are both welcome.' He called to one of the warriors: 'Endan, look to our guests,' then led me away towards the feast-hall. 'I'm glad you're here,' he went on. 'I'm trying to persuade Cairenn's father to let me have her as my bride and I need you to sing a song about how brave I am. Somebody has to.'

'Surely he won't refuse the king's son?' I said, jabbing him in the ribs. He stopped short and I heard my own words and cursed myself.

'The king's brother,' he corrected me.

'How goes it with Owain?'

He shook his head and looked down at his feet. 'Strangely, at the moment. I was about to set out for Bryneich when he rode in from Strathclud, having parted with Riderch and Echu. He blames himself for leaving our father's work undone and Aethelric free in Metcaud, but Riderch was mourning his son, Echu had lost so many of his band at Dun Guayrdi, what else could he do but come back? The news here is none too cheerful; Dunaut has been raiding cattle in the south so Llywarch has ridden to harry Pennuin, and Owain sits here worrying about Cugaun in atraeth and how to help him.'

'What happened in Manau Goddodin?'

'That's the only good news. Morcant is food for the ravens, and his vile harper with him. The kingship has been taken by a man who sounds worthy named Rhufawn, and he has given Owain his pledge of friendship.'

'Surely,' I said, 'that means we can begin again, and stronger, without Morcant to stab us in the back?'

'No,' said Pascent. 'We seem to have the promise of war with Dunaut, and the Eingl of Deur may well be mustering to take revenge for what happened at Catraeth, and then again . . .' he paused, 'why should men follow Owain where our father failed?' He clapped his hand on my shoulder again and we passed through the doorway of the hall. 'Go and see Owain for yourself. He's in the courtyard of the fountain, and he'll be glad to see you.'

I padded across the fine Roman floor to draw back the leather curtain of the far doorway. In the courtyard beyond Owain sat with his back against the wall, playing with the ears of his wolf-hound, and Branwen sat weaving at a loom. They rose to their feet when they saw me and were both at a loss for words, so I walked across to them joking: 'Why is it that whenever a harper returns to Caer Lugualid he is stared at like a ghost?'

'Thank Christos you're safe,' said Owain. 'Is Myrddin . . . with you?'

'Only his spirit. The man is gone beyond the sunset.'

'Tell me what happened.' We squatted down on the paving stones and Branwen glided away into the hall. I began to tell Owain what had happened to me since we parted in Bryneich. He now wore the gold circlet of kingship about his brow, but he had also changed in subtler ways; the laughter seemed to have gone out of his face for its place to be taken by a cold energy of alertness. I had finished the telling of Myrddin's death and told of my journey when Branwen returned with a bowl of yellow mead and offered it to me. The laughter had gone out of her, too, but it only sharpened her red-gold beauty. I took the mead, trying to imagine what Myrddin would have said, and scraped together a handful of words as I raised the bowl in salutation.

'To the memory of Urien your father, and to the strength of the kingdom he left to you.'

Owain drank after me, then passed the bowl to Branwen who withdrew. 'Tell me,' said Owain, 'did Myrddin say anything about the way things turned in Bryneich?'

'Only that your father would sooner have died on a war trail of his own choosing than wait in Rheged till the Eingl hunted him down like a boar in a thicket.'

'He did not say what he thought I should do?'

'No.'

Owain looked down at the brindled head of the wolfhound lying in his lap. 'Did he say what he thought you should do?'

'He told me to keep the harp, to ask Llywarch to continue my teaching or to go and learn from the harpers of Gwynedd.'

He nodded and looked up at me. 'I had hoped you would stay and be my harper.'

'I am your harper, Owain. I would have no harp at all if you had not found me in the mists five summers ago and brought me to Caer Lugualid. When I travel to learn my craft it will be with your leave, but not without it.'

A trace of the old smile creased his face. 'Oh you will have my leave to travel and to learn your craft. I want the best harper in the north.'

'And I will always return,' I replied, 'because I want the best king in the north.'

He groaned. 'Are you so sure I can ever be that?'

'If you try to be a king such as your father was, and I try to be a harper such as Myrddin was, then assuredly we will in time be the best king and the best harper in the north, as they were.'

The vague smile returned. 'If only because we are the last king and the last harper. . . . Tell me something. When we reached Bryneich and you felt you had to ride ahead to Caer Brighid, it was as though something called you and something waited to be discovered. At the time I took it as a good omen, but since our dreams failed I have often wondered what it can have been that called you so strongly that night. Did you discover anything on those hills?'

It was my turn to smile. 'Not what I thought I would find, but it was still a good omen. I discovered I had a friend to ride with me.'

When evening came I ate with my own kin, with Cialgrin and Fionn. They had welcomed Uaran and Emer and invited them to look over the rest of the crumbling Roman house and choose rooms to clear out and make their own, so there were six of us round the hearth. My uncle sprawled against the wall, his gashed leg stretched in front of him, and I sat by him to talk of how things had been in Caer Brighid. The wound had been hard on him and

poke of remembering little between leaving Bryneich in the
ule cart and coming to his senses days later by his own hearth.
Little Dichuil charged from one to another of us like a war horse,
amazed at having three visitors to make a fuss of him.

Cialgrin did not speak of how he felt about the riding to
Bryneich, except to say one thing as I rose to leave at the end of
the evening. 'You must write a song about the taking of Dun
Guayrdi. We will never see a battle like that again, and it is a song
Talhearn would be glad of.'

I brooded on this as I made my way through the streets to the
feast-hall, enjoying the freshness of the night air after the heat
around the fire. I had not touched my harp since before Urien's
death, and I had not pulled Myrddin's from its calfskin bag since I
took it from his side. There was not one song I felt like singing. It
was as though my gift had left me, and I had become useless to the
Moon.

Pascent woke me the next morning, and as I sat up aching from
the riding of the last few days I saw that the hall was busy with
people packing bundles.

'What is it?' I asked. 'Is Aethelric coming?'

'If he is he won't find us here,' laughed Pascent. 'It's Midsummer Eve and Owain wants to pass the solstice in Echwyd.'

I rubbed my eyes. My head felt like a roasted chicken. I had
often heard of Echwyd, Urien's steading among the Lake Mountains, and known he and his sons go there to hunt. 'When will you
be back?' I asked.

'Whenever you are. You're coming with us. You're one of the
king's companions now.'

We took the road south from Caer Lugualid, a small group of
twelve riders. Branwen came with us, riding beside Owain wearing a pair of breeks and with her hair plaited and pinned behind
her head. When we reached the rath the Romans called Voreda
we turned south-west and followed a road which led up into the
low hills of the eastern edge of the Lake Mountains. The hills
were green and rounded, altogether like the hills of Bryneich. It
could have made me weep but instead it made my heart soar to be
among hills once more. By midday we were riding down the
headwaters of the Vale of Echwyd, past the shells of Roman raths
where the road ended and on by older trackways which laced
through the woods and pastures of the valley floor.

To our right rose the steep sides of the largest mountain I had
ever seen, a wide wall broken only by spattering streams like

trails of sour milk, streaked with long screes where even bracken could not grow. I stared up at it, dizzy at the sense of its immensity and power. I turned to Pascent, who was riding beside me.

'Has it a name?' I asked, pointing upwards.

'Blencathra,' he replied. 'See, we have almost arrived.' He pointed to the southern side of the valley, where gentler slopes rose towards hills which were even higher if less sheer. Above the valley, on a knoll beside which another white stream pitched down, was the timbered earthwork of a dun. As we crossed the valley floor and began the climb towards it, Pascent told me how it was still called Dun Cynvarch after his grandfather.

'Why was it never Dun Urien?' I asked.

'Because it has always carried the name of its master, and my father never had time to become its master. My grandfather fell at Arderydd with Gwendolleu, who was his cousin, and when the kingship passed to my father it dragged him to Caer Lugualid where Gwendolleu had ruled. He was always happiest here. We are all of us happiest here.'

As we rode into the dun, to be met by the bleating of sheep and the smell of peatsmoke and to dismount and see the Vale of Echwyd stretched out beneath us, I found that easy to understand. We were greeted by the handful of men whose life was the tending of the flocks, herds and pastures of Echwyd, but we were welcomed into the house itself by an old, heavy, smiling woman named Drusticca with a face as wrinkled as a walnut. She had been Urien's nurse, then the nurse of his children who she now greeted as her own and led into the hearth she kept for them. I imagined how she must wonder what they were doing and long for their return, and I thought of my mother by her own lonely hearth. Drusticca had the pain of knowing that neither Urien nor Elphin would ever return, but she swallowed it and concentrated on the three who remained to her.

Owain and Pascent took what was left of the afternoon to ride out to see their horse and cattle herds and to join in the driving of them to the stone circle further down the valley where later that evening we would gather to light the Midsummer fires, and later still drive the animals between the fires to summon fertility for them. I could have ridden with them but pleaded the need to rest after so much journeying. I sat for a while in the yard listening to Drusticca and Branwen talking; Drusticca wanted to hear all about Cairenn, whom Pascent had nearly brought with us, and Branwen wanted to talk of how they had all been when they were

...i. Neither of them spoke of what had happened over the last
months, perhaps because they could not bear to.

After a while I wandered down to the gateway of the dun and
sat with my back against the earthwork looking up at the rubbled
mass of Blencathra. I imagined Urien as a boy, growing up here in
Echwyd, knowing only that this was his land and never dreaming
that he would be king of Rheged and take a war trail to the other
side of Britain to die so far from his own hills. I thought of my
own undreamt-of pattern, the journey in the other direction
which had brought me to Echwyd, as strangely distant from Caer
Brighid as Bryneich must have seemed to Urien.

On all of this Blencathra looked down with supreme indiffer-
ence. It was nothing to her what happened to the children of Echwyd; they could fail or succeed, survive or die and she would still
look down with the same impassivity. When Outigern and Bryneich are forgotten Yr Cerrid will still bulk the skyline, though I
imagine the Eingl will give her another name, and she will have
yet another when they are gone and the names Aethelric and
Bernicia have themselves become meaningless. By that time I
expect also that the names Urien and Rheged will mean nothing,
unless. . . .

The shadows were already lengthening down in the valley, for
here in Echwyd the sun sinks behind the mountains while the sky
is still light. There was a long evening ahead. Soon Owain and
Pascent would return and we would set out for the stone circle
and the Midsummer fires. I had not much time if I wanted to have
a song ready to sing at the firelighting, so I lurched to my feet,
cursing my aches, and began to run towards the house where I
had left the harp. Already the whisper of a tune and a cluster of
words were making a pattern in my head. I would sing of the
taking of Dun Guayrdi, I would sing of the riding of Urien.